THE
Rest
of Us
JUST
LIVE
HERE

ALSO BY PATRICK NESS

More Than This

The Crane Wife

A Monster Calls

Monsters of Men

The Ask and the Answer

The Knife of Never Letting Go

Topics About Which I Know Nothing

The Crash of Hennington

First published 2015 by Walker Books Ltd
87 Vauxhall Walk, London SE11 5HJ

2 4 6 8 10 9 7 5 3 1

This book has been typeset in Sabon and Futura

Printed and bound in Great Britain by Clays Ltd, St Ives plc

British Library Cataloguing in Publication Data:
a catalogue record for this book is available from the British Library

ISBN 978-1-4063-3116-5 (Hardback)
ISBN 978-1-4063-6747-8 (Exclusive)
ISBN 978-1-4063-6179-7 (Trade paperback)

www.walker.co.uk

THE *Rest of Us* JUST LIVE HERE

PATRICK NESS

WALKER
BOOKS

For my own excellent sister,
Melissa Anne Brown,
who's both kind and funny,
the best possible combination

I thought I could organise freedom.

How Scandinavian of me.

–Björk

CHAPTER THE FIRST, *in which the Messenger of the Immortals arrives in a surprising shape, looking for a permanent Vessel; and after being chased by her through the woods, indie kid Finn meets his final fate.*

◄O►

On the day we're the last people to see indie kid Finn alive, we're all sprawled together in the Field, talking about love and stomachs.

"I don't believe that, though," my sister says, and I look up at the slight tension in her voice. She gives me a half-annoyed nod of reassurance in the sunshine, then shakes her head again at Henna. "You *always* have a choice. I don't care if you think it's love – and by the way, NOT a word you should throw around so easily – but even if that, even if that word, you can still choose to act right."

"I said I loved the way he *looked*," Henna says. "I didn't say I loved *him*. You're twisting my words. And that's not what I'm talking about anyway. I'm talking about ... how your heart fills up. Actually, no, it's not even your heart, it's your *stomach*. You feel it and everything just *goes*."

"No, it doesn't," my sister says, firmly. "No. It. Doesn't."

"Mel–"

"You can feel it, and you can still do the right thing."

Henna frowns. "Why is it a question of the 'right thing'? I'm describing a totally normal human feeling. Nathan's a hot guy."

I look back down at my History textbook. I touch each of the four corners, counting silently to myself. I see Jared notice.

"You said you had no choice," Mel pursues. "You said if you'd been able to kiss him, you would have done it right there, regardless of who saw. Or if he had a girlfriend already. Or if Tony was around–"

"I'm not going out with Tony any more–"

"Yeah, but you know how sensitive he is. You'd

THE REST OF US JUST LIVE HERE

have hurt him and then you'd have said you had no choice and it would have been bullshit."

Henna puts her hands over her face in frustration. *"Melinda—"*

"It's something I feel strongly about."

"I can see that—"

"And don't call me Melinda."

"Henna's right, though," Jared says, from where he's lying back with his head on Henna's butt. "It is in your stomach."

"On a guy, you'd think it'd be lower," Mel says.

"That's different," Jared says, sitting up. "Your dick or whatever, that's just *wanting*. Animal stuff. This is more."

"Yeah," Henna agrees.

"You feel it right here." Jared puts his hand on his belly. It's a biggish kind of belly and we know he doesn't draw attention to it lightly. "And it's like, for that moment, everything you believed is wrong. Or doesn't matter. And everything that was complicated is suddenly, like, yes-and-no simple, because your stomach is really the boss and it's telling you that your desire is possible and that it's not the answer to everything but it's the one thing that's going to make the questions more bearable."

He stops, looking up into the sun. We all know what he means. *He* knows we all know what he means. He never really talks about it, though. We wish he did.

"Your stomach isn't the boss of you," Mel says, evenly.

"Oh," Jared says, realizing. "Sorry–"

Mel shakes her head, brushing it off. "Not what I meant. Your heart isn't the boss of you either. Thinks it is. Isn't. You can *always* choose. Always."

"You can't choose not to feel," Henna says.

"But you can choose how to act."

"Yeah," Jared says. "Hard, though."

"Early Christians thought your soul was in your stomach," I say.

There's a silence as a new wind blows across the grass, all by its lonesome, as if saying, *Don't mind me.*

"Dad told me once," I say.

Mel looks down to her laptop and starts typing in more homework answers. "And what would Dad know, I wonder," she says.

The wind picks up a little more (*Terribly sorry*, I imagine it saying; apparently, the wind is British, wondering how it got all the way over here) and Henna has to snap her hand down on a page of an assignment that's threatening to fly away. "Why do we even have paper any more?"

"Books," Jared says.

"Toilet paper," Mel says.

"Because paper is a thing," I say, "and sometimes you need things rather than just thoughts."

"I wasn't really looking for an answer," Henna says, tucking the page – a handout on the Civil War that we've all got – under her computer tablet.

I tap the four corners of my textbook again, counting silently in my head. And again. And one more time. I see Jared watching me but pretending not to. Another gust of British wind tousles my hair. (*Top of the morning!* Oh, no, wait, that's Irish.) It's a sunny day for it to be so windy all of a sudden. We only come out here when the weather's nice enough, and it's been a weirdly warm April and early May. The Field isn't really much of a field, it's more like a property plot that someone never built on because they died or lost it in a divorce or something, a big grassy square at the end of the road from my house with some handy sawn-off tree stumps scattered here and there. Rows of trees block it off from the rest of everything else, too. You'd have to make a point of coming back here to know about it, which nobody does as we're so far out in the boonies it's only actual super-thick forest beyond anyway. You can hear coyotes at night and we get deer in our yard all the time.

"Hey," Jared says, "anyone doing the Reconstruction After the Civil War essay or is it just me?"

"I am," I say.

"You are?" Mel says, distressed. "I'm doing it, too."

"Me, too," Henna says.

"*Everyone?*" Jared says.

Mel looks at me. "Could you not? I mean, could you really, really not?"

"I've got all these notes, though–" I say.

"But I'm really good on the Reconstruction."

"So do the Reconstruction essay–"

"We can't *both* do it. Yours will be all brainiac and I'll look stupid by comparison."

My sister always does this. She thinks she's stupid. She's so, so not.

"It'll be better than *mine*," Jared says.

"Mikey, just let me do it." And here, I know, most people would be thinking, *Bossy older sister*, and most people who don't know us would be wondering why we're both seniors even though she's more than a year older than me and most people would think they could hear a spoiled tone in her voice.

Most people would be wrong. She's not whining. She's asking, kinda nicely for her. And most people wouldn't see the fear in her eyes over this exam.

But I can.

"Okay," I say. "I'll do Causes of the Civil War."

She nods her head in thanks. She turns to Henna. "Could you do Causes, too?"

"Hey!" Jared says. "What about me?"

"Seriously?" Mel says to him.

"Nah, not seriously," he laughs. Jared, despite being big and tall and shaving by age eleven and a linebacker on the football team since we were all freshman, is a math guy. Give him numbers, he's great. Give him words and sentences to put together and his forehead creases down so you can see exactly what he'll look like when he's eighty.

"Mel," Henna says. "You gotta stop–"

Which is when one of the indie kids comes running out of the treeline, his old-timey jacket flapping out behind him. He pushes his fashionably black-rimmed glasses back on his nose and runs past about twenty feet from where we're all tumbled together. He doesn't see us – the indie kids never really see us, not even when we're sitting next to them in class – just crosses the Field and disappears into the opposite treeline, which we all know only leads to deeper forest.

There's a silent few seconds where we all exchange wtf glances and then a young girl glowing with her own light comes running out of the woods from where the indie kid came. She doesn't see us either, though she's so bright we all have to shade our eyes, and then she disappears into the second treeline, too.

None of us says anything for a minute, then Jared asks, "Was that Finn?"

"Which Finn?" my sister says. "Aren't all the indie kids called Finn?"

"I think there are a couple Dylans," Henna says, "and a Nash."

"There are two Satchels, I know that," I say. "A boy Satchel and a girl Satchel."

"It was one of the Finns," Jared says. "I'm pretty sure."

A pillar of blue light, bright enough to see even in the sunshine, shoots up suddenly from a point where the indie kid (I think Jared's right, it *was* one of the ones called Finn) and the glowing girl might have run.

"What are they doing *now*?" Mel says. "What was with the little girl?"

"And the lights?" I say.

"They better not blow up the high school again," Jared says. "My cousin had to have his graduation ceremony in a parking lot."

"Do you think Nathan is an indie kid?" Henna asks, making Mel groan.

"The name could go either way," Jared says, watching the pillar glow.

"What kind of a guy transfers to a new school five weeks before the end of his senior year?" I ask, trying not to make it sound like anything, tapping the corners of my textbook again.

"The kind of guy that Henna falls in love with," Mel says.

"OH MY GOD I DIDN'T SAY LOVE!" Henna shouts.

Mel grins. "You sure seem to have a lot of passion about the subject, though. Or is that just your stomach talking?"

The wind stops, all of a sudden.

"Light's gone," Jared says. The pillar of light has faded. We can't hear the sound of anyone running any more. We watch the woods, not sure what to expect, then we all jump when my sister's laptop starts playing a song we like. It's an alarm she set. It means our parents have left our house for the evening to go visit our grandmother.

It means it's safe to go home.

CHAPTER THE SECOND, *in which indie kid Satchel writes a poem, and her mom and dad give her loving space to just feel what she needs to; then an indie kid called Dylan arrives at her house, terrified, to say a mysterious glowing girl has informed him of the death of indie kid Finn; Satchel and Dylan comfort each other, platonically.*

◄O►

Over the course of my life, I've told Henna about my mad, desperate feelings for her exactly zero times.

We've got a lot in common: a thing with anxiety we don't really like to talk about, best friends who we kind of love more than any girlfriend or boyfriend could really compete with, parents who … aren't the best. We've got Mel in common, of course, so that's good, and we're also both not indie kids, even though she's totally got an indie kid name (but it's because her dad is foreign, so it doesn't count; and I guess in Finland, "Henna" isn't very indie kid anyway. Plus her last name is impossible).

We've been friends since we were eight, over half my life now, though mostly with my sister as an intermediary. I've been madly, desperately in love with Henna from when we were about twelve. She started dating Tony Kim slightly before then, which was, of course, the thing that made me realize the madly, desperately thing. She broke up with Tony this past New Year and has been single since then. It's now May.

So what have I been doing for the last five months? I refer you to "zero times" above.

"Coast is clear," Mel says, as the four of us come down our driveway, dogs barking eternally in distant yards, and see my mom's car gone. We live in a suburb of a suburb of a suburb of a suburb of a city that takes about an hour to get to. There's nothing out here but woods and the huge great Mountain on the very near horizon that'll blow up one day and flatten everyone and everything in this part of the state. That could happen tomorrow. It could happen five thousand years from now. Life, eh?

The road to our house only got properly paved last year, and our neighbours are a mixture of professionals like my parents who wanted a bit of land to build a house on and other people who think Fox News is too liberal and build bunkers for their guns. Out here, people either grow organic turnips or vast fields of marijuana. My parents do daffodils.

Don't walk on them. I mean, seriously, don't walk on them.

Henna's parents live down the road, but that's coincidence because we actually know them from the church both our families have gone to for a hundred years. Henna's mom is the music minister there. She and Henna are the only black people in the whole church. That's our tiny bit of the world for you. Henna's dad is a white Finnish foot doctor (so, like, *really* white) who does mission trips to Africa with Henna's mom. That's where Henna is going to spend this summer, the last summer she could spend with her high school friends before leaving for (a very Christian) college. She's going to be in the Central

African Republic, speaking high school French to Central African Republicans who are going to get foot doctoring and music ministry whether they want to or not.

What this means is that five months of a last chance since her break-up with Tony has narrowed down to four and a half weeks of a last chance until graduation. Given my success rate to date, I don't think my odds are very good.

Mel lets us in the house, and we aren't two steps inside before Mary Magdalene, our tubby little orange cat, is running a purring streak around Jared's legs. He touches her nose lightly with his finger. "I see you," he whispers, and Mary Mags does an ecstatic lopsided spin to the floor, like a falling propeller.

"Anyone want anything?" Mel says, heading to the kitchen.

Jared asks for an energy drink. Henna asks for an energy drink. I ask for an energy drink. "Little help?" Mel calls from the kitchen. I go over. I look at the glass of water she's poured herself. "I'm fine," she says quietly. "We're out of Diet Coke and I hate the taste of those things." She's got a point about the energy drinks, which are all called Monstropop or Rev or Lotusexxy and which are, yeah, kinda disgusting, but so filled with caffeine I'm unlikely to sleep until college.

We're next to the fridge. I open the door. There's a bottle of Diet Coke in the back. It only has a little bit in it, but still.

"Mikey," she whispers.

I look into her eyes.

"Sometimes it's just hard," she says. "It doesn't mean anything. And you saw me at lunch."

I did see her at lunch. And she's right, it was fine. Home is always harder for her.

I tap the rims of each of the four glasses in turn with my fingers. I tap them again. "Dammit," I whisper, and tap them again. Mel just waits. Three times seems to be enough, so I shut the fridge door and help her take the drinks out to the couches.

"What do you think that was in the Field?" asks Henna, looking worried. "With the indie kid?"

"I hope nothing," Mel says. "And even if it is something, they'd better hold off until after graduation."

"I just mean I hope he's okay," Henna says, and we all can tell she's thinking of her brother.

The indie kids, huh? You've got them at your school, too. That group with the cool-geek haircuts and the charity shop clothes and names from the fifties. Nice enough, never mean, but always the ones who end up being the Chosen One when the vampires come calling or when the alien queen needs the Source of All Light or something. They're too cool to ever, ever do anything like go to prom or listen to music other than jazz while reading poetry. They've always got some story going on that they're heroes of. The rest of us just have to live here, hovering around the edges, left out of it all, for the most part.

Having said that, the indie kids do die a lot. Which must suck.

"Where's Merde Breath?" Jared asks, changing the subject. Our little sister, Meredith (and yes, I know, Michael and Melinda and Meredith and even Mary Magdalene the cat. We once even had a Labrador called Martha, but she bit a porcupine one day and that was the end of that. Apparently you *can* put a price on love. It's slightly less than $1,200 for doggy face surgery).

Anyway.

Meredith is ten, a loon, maybe a genius (our mom

is certainly counting on it), and is hopelessly, painfully ensnared by Bolts of Fire, the country and western boy band specifically created to hopelessly and painfully ensnare ten-year-old girls, even the geniuses. She's played their biggest song, "Bold Sapphire" (by Bolts of Fire, get it?), exactly 1,157 times. I know, because I checked, after begging my parents for mercy from having to hear it a 1,158th. We're all a little obsessive, us Mitchell kids.

Jared is a firm second in her affections after Bolts of Fire, though. He's big, he's friendly, and there's the whole cat deal. If there's one thing we all, every one of us, agree on, it's that Jared is going to be a great dad.

Not that any of us have first-hand experience of one, really, except Jared, which figures.

"German lessons," I tell him. "My mom didn't think she was being challenged enough at school."

Jared blinks. "She's ten."

"They're still hoping they've got one left who isn't screwed-up," Mel says, flicking on a downloaded TV programme we've all already seen as background noise.

Henna looks at me. "You're not screwed-up."

"No one in this family is screwed-up," says our

mother, coming through the front door. "That's the official campaign line and we're sticking to it."

She drops her purse on the table by the door, already frowning at the four teenagers draped across her couches. She's two hours early. "Hello, everyone," she practically booms, seeming friendly enough, though Mel and I can already tell we're going to pay for this later. "Look at all the feet up on the furniture."

Jared and Henna slowly put their feet on the floor.

"Hello, State Senator," Jared says, politely.

"Just 'Senator' is the protocol, Jared," my mom says with a tight smile, "even for a lowly state government official. As I'm sure you must know by now. Hello, Henna."

"Mrs Mitchell," Henna greets, her voice three sizes smaller than a minute ago.

"You're early," Mel says.

"Yes," my mom says. "I can see how you might think that."

"Where's Dad?" I ask.

"Still with your grandma."

"How is she?"

Mom's smile gets even tighter. "You two staying for dinner?" she asks Jared and Henna, somehow communicating clearly that they're not actually invited.

"No, thank you," Jared says, getting up, downing his energy drink in one. "We were just heading out."

"You don't have to leave on my account," my mom says, meaning that yes, yes, they do.

"Homework," Henna says, gathering her things quickly. She leaves her energy drink on the coffee table. It's already sweating beads of water down the side, and I can feel my heart start to race at the need to either put a coaster underneath it or wipe the water away or something.

One glass of energy drink. One.

Mel sees me staring at the glass, picks it up off the table, and drinks it down, even though she particularly hates Lotusexxy.

I give her a pleading look of thanks.

While I've been trapped, Jared and Henna are at the door already, waving their goodbyes. The door shuts behind them. It's just us family now. Embrace the warmth.

"It's bad enough you're friends with that boy–" my mom starts.

I get up so fast, she stops mid-sentence. I don't put on my jacket. I don't take anything with me except the car keys I've already got in my pocket. I'm out the door before she can do anything more than give me a shocked look.

I catch Jared and Henna out on the walk. "Ride home?" I say.

It takes about three seconds to drop Henna off down the street, though I do get a full eye-contact thank you from her as she gets out. My mad, desperate head thinks of mad, desperate things to say to her, but of course I don't. Then Jared and I are driving, even though his own car is still parked at my house. I turn the opposite direction from where he lives.

He says nothing.

We drive until the sun sets. There are more back roads into and out of these woods than anyone can count, than are probably on any map. You can drive and drive and drive and just see forest and fields, the occasional cow, the occasional elk, the even more occasional moose (the animal Patron Saint of Perpetual Embarrassment; I can relate, though not to being Catholic, which I've apparently decided mooses are). The Mountain glows in and out of view, turning pink, then blue, then shadow, as it watches us wander.

I finally stop in a turn-off by a glacial lake. Huge, crystal clear, cold as death.

"Is it Henna?" Jared finally asks.

"It's not Henna," I say, into the dark. "Well, it is. But not just that. And not my parents either."

"Good, because I'm fine about that. The bad feeling between me and your mom is entirely mutual."

I stare out into the really amazingly dark night. There are more stars over my part of the world than anywhere else I've ever seen. "Four and a half weeks to go."

"Four and a half weeks," Jared agrees. "Graduation."

He waits. I wait, too. After a long minute, I turn on the cabin light and hold up my hands to him. "What am I looking at?" he asks.

I point to my fingertips. They're wrinkled and cracked. "Eczema."

"And?"

I turn off the cabin light. "I washed my hands seventeen times this morning after taking a piss before History."

Jared exhales a long, long time. "Dude."

I just swallow. It's loud in the silence. "I think it's starting again."

"It's probably just the pressure of everything," Jared offers. "Finals, your massively unrequited love for Henna–"

"Don't say unrequited."

"...your massively *invisible* love for Henna..."

I hit him on the arm. It's friendly. More silence.

"What if I go crazy?" I finally whisper.

I feel Jared shrug. "At least it'll piss off the Senator."

We laugh. A little.

"You won't, Mikey," he says. "And if you do, I'll be there to pull you back."

Which makes me feel...

Okay, look, Jared likes guys. We all know it,

he's told us, even though he's never officially had a boyfriend (because who the hell is he going to meet out here who isn't a creepy old farmer?) and he never really talks about it or what he gets up to on those weekend evenings when we know he's not working, but still says he can't come out with us. And fine, he and I have messed around a few times growing up together, even though I like girls, even though I like *Henna*, because a horny teenage boy would do it with a tree trunk if it offered at the right moment, but you're going to have to hear this the right way when I tell you that I love exactly three people in the entire world, excluding whatever this is with Henna.

Three people. Mel. Meredith. And the third person isn't either of my parents.

"You want to talk crazy?" Jared says.

"Yeah," I say. "Yeah, I know."

There's so much crazy in this world, my counting and hand-washing and door-locking and checking and tapping can seem like raging mental health by comparison. Jared's crazy is way crazier than mine, though I don't think his makes him lie awake at night in bed, thinking it'd be easier if he was–

You know.

And if you don't know, you don't want to.

"There's a mountain lion out there," Jared says, looking out his window.

I sigh. "There's always a mountain lion out there."

CHAPTER THE THIRD, *in which indie kid Finn's body is discovered; Satchel – who once dated Finn – asks Dylan and a second indie kid also called Finn to skip school and help her talk to her alcoholic uncle, who is the lead police officer investigating the death; meanwhile, the Messenger, inside a new Vessel, is already among them, preparing the way for the arrival of the Immortals.*

◄O►

Our town is just like your town. Schools, family-themed restaurants, lots of cars. There's a bunch of huge churches clustered together, trying to blend in with all the family-themed restaurants, because salvation is as easy as chicken wings, I guess. We've got fire stations with signs that tell you when burning season begins and ends. We've got sheriff's offices with signs that tell you to Buckle Up. We've got a lumber yard with signs that tell you angry right-wing puns. We've got RV lots, banks, a Walmart, a couple multiplexes.

We've got trees. So many trees. Everything here used to be a forest, after all.

And yeah, so fine, our part of town has more than its fair share of trees and less than its fair share of multiplexes, but don't look down on us. It was just as bad here as it was for you when the indie kids were battling the undead in our neck of the woods (though that was just after I was born, so I only know about it from my Uncle Rick, who doesn't get invited around very much any more). We had the same amount of heartache when a new round of indie kids exorcized the sorrow from all those soul-eating ghosts eight years later (that was the year they blew up the high school, a heretofore unknown part of the exorcism ritual, I guess). And don't even get me started on when the indie kids fell in love with and then defeated all the vampires a few years back. Henna's older brother Teemu got mixed up with them and pretty much vanished one day. They haven't seen him since, though he writes the occasional email. Always at night.

And we *dream* the same in my town as you probably do in a city. We yearn the same, wish the same. We're just as screwed-up and brave and false and loyal and wrong and right as anyone else. And even if there's no one in my family or my circle of friends who's going to be the Chosen One or the Beacon of Peace or whatever the hell it's going to be next time around, I reckon there are a lot more people like me than there are indie kids with unusual names and capital-D Destinies (though I'm being mean here; they're often quite nice, the indie kids, just ... they've got a clan and they're sticking to it).

Me, all I want to do is graduate. And have a last summer with my friends. And go away to college. And (more than) kiss Henna (more than) once. And then get on with finding out about the rest of my life.

Don't you?

"Did you get in trouble?" Jared asks the next morning as we sit down in the back row of a Calculus class that he's already got so much extra-credit in he could skip the final and still get an A.

"Just the weekly lecture on how keeping a united family front is more important than usual in an election year, blah blah blah." I glance at him. "You were mentioned."

He grins. "I bet."

The school bell goes as the classroom door opens a last time, and Nathan comes in.

"Sorry," he says, flashing a smile at Ms Johnson, the Calculus teacher. She's this really smart, funny older lesbian so the smile totally shouldn't work on her. Somehow it still does.

I count out the four corners of my desk. Seven times.

"Dude," Jared whispers. "It's just a guy. He's not the Devil."

"Henna likes him."

"She said he was pretty. He is."

I stop counting.

"Well, he is," Jared shrugs. "Just calling the facts."

"Yeah, but why would you transfer into a new school five weeks before–"

The intercom system crackles. *Attention students,*

I guess, says our Principal. He's French Canadian and no matter what he says, he always sounds like he's dying of boredom. *I have some troubling and sad news that some of you will have already seen on social media, no doubt. I am afraid that the body of one of our seniors, Finn Brinkman, was found this morning. There are, as yet, no leads to the cause of his death, but we urge all students to take extra care, to not travel alone, and to report anything suspicious to the authorities. Counselling is available in the office should you need it or something.*

Calculus has fallen silent. I turn to Jared. I know he's thinking the same thing I'm thinking.

"We should tell someone," I say.

"Yep," he says. "Won't do any good."

No. No, it probably won't.

"Well, that was a waste of a morning," Mel says, as we gather for lunch. We've taken senior privilege and all piled into my car to go to the Mexican fast-food place around the hill next to the school, even though we're lucky to have gotten a lunch break at all.

We'd all met in the office and told the Vice Principal – who, like all Vice Principals, is genetically Nazi – what we'd seen. He eventually called *one* cop whose breath was as thick with booze as my father's is in the evening. That cop proceeded to not believe a word we said about seeing Finn running through the Field, the glowing girl running after him, or the blue pillar of light that rose and then faded. He basically yelled at us for wasting his time.

Okay, fine, so Finn's body wasn't found anywhere *near* there, but I just can't believe the things that people won't believe. Or the things people won't even *see*. I was in the ninth grade when the vampires came. But even though people started dying, even though people disappeared and stayed gone, even though you could point at one and say, "That's a vampire," most people, most *adults*, still don't believe it ever happened.

What happens to you when you get older? Do you just *forget* everything from before you turned eighteen? Do you *make* yourself forget? I mean the cop was old enough to have been a teenager when the whole soul-eating ghost thing was happening, so did he just block it out of his mind? Did he talk himself into not believing it actually happened? Convince himself it was a virus, that the explosion at the old high school was a gas leak? Or is it that he thought what happened to him was so original, so life-changing and harrowing and amazing, that there's no way he could ever imagine it happening to anyone else?

It's not every adult, I know, but still, we see a guy the day he dies and the half-drunk policeman in charge threatens to arrest *us*.

Honestly. Adults. How do they live in the world?

(Or maybe that *is* how they live in the world.)

"I told you we shouldn't bother," Henna says, sitting next to me, thinking nothing of it. "When Teemu disappeared, the police did exactly nothing. Said he was old enough to make his own choices."

"At least you still hear from him," Mel says, gently. "Once in a while."

Henna shakes her head, like that doesn't help, which of course it doesn't. "I think it's why my mom and dad go on all these mission trips. Try to beat some of the darkness out of the world with their bare hands."

She makes this sound both impressive and a sad, sad waste of time. There's also pity. They did lose their son. The Silvennoinens are as complicated as anyone else. More, if you count trying to say their last name out loud.

I touch all of the pointed ends of the tortilla bowl they've fried to put my taco stuff in. There are twelve, just like on a clock, which is so pleasing, I only have to count it once. I glance over at Mel's plate. She's got some salad and some plain chicken, so that's fine, and I heard her order a Diet Coke, also good. She hates having people watch her eat, though, so I make a point to look away, as do Henna and Jared.

"I just hope whatever it is gets finished by graduation–" Jared says.

"Weird about that dead kid, huh?" says a voice.

Nathan's standing there with a tray. And surprisingly, he looks genuinely spooked.

"Hey," Henna says, a little too brightly. "You want to join us?"

Mel and Jared scoot up to make room, so now I'm sitting across from him. Hooray. "I don't think we've really met," he says to me. "Nathan."

"I know who you are," I say, but I do shake his hand. I'm not *that* rude.

"This guy who died, though," he says, and his eyes are still slightly wide. "Did any of you know him?"

"He was an indie kid," Mel says, "so not really."

Nathan stares down at his enchilada for a second. Henna and Jared watch him, openly. Mel takes the opportunity to eat more of her chicken. I study Nathan, too. I can't see what Henna likes at all. His hair's that stupid forward swoosh-mess that looks like it's eating his brain. His clothes are a kind of noncommittal faded blue. His eyes are dark enough to be black and his earlobes, when he brushes his hair out of the way, are scarred from where he obviously once had sprocket earrings before having them sewn up again.

Idiot. Moron. I hate you.

"So you're from Tulsa?" Henna asks, and I start tucking into my lunch.

"Yeah," Nathan says, smiling faintly. "Before that, Portland. Before that, Fort Knox, Kentucky–"

"Army dad?" Jared asks.

"Army mom," Nathan answers. "Dad stayed in Florida. Five postings ago."

"Must suck," I say, trying to keep any heat out of my voice. "Moving to a new school five weeks before graduation."

He runs a hand through that mop of hair. "Little bit," he says, meaning a lot. "And a kid dies my first week." He glances around the table. "Not that that's in any way suspicious."

He smiles. The others laugh. "But wow, though," he says, more quietly. "I hope whatever it is this time isn't too bad."

My phone buzzes, two seconds before Mel's does, too. We both look.

BOLTSOFFIREBOLTSOFFIREBOLTSOFFIRE!!!!! COMING TO FAIR!!!! I'LL DIE IF I CANT GO!!!! PLEASE CONVINCE MOM!!! PLEASEPLEASEPLEASEPLEASEPLEASE PLEASEPLEASE!!!!!! Love, Meredith.

"That can't be right," I say, showing the others the text. "Bolts of Fire? At our crappy little county fair?"

"Yeah," Henna says. "I saw it online somewhere.

They're coming for some little girl's cancer last wish or something."

Nathan's staring at us. "You guys aren't ... *fans* or anything?"

"All right," I say, later that night, putting extra slices of cheesy toast on a plate for the really, really fat family at table two. "He *is* pretty."

"And nice," Jared says, dumping sprigs of parsley on our waiting orders. "And a little bit tragic."

"And new." I heap the plates up on my tray. Jared does the same for his section. "I don't stand a chance, do I?"

"You've got the same chance you've always had, my friend," he says, and disappears into his half of the restaurant. We work at Grillers, a steakhouse for cheap dates. The kind of place with all-you-can-eat shrimp, all-you-can-eat fries, and all-you-can-eat cheesy toast, which, to be fair, is really awesome cheesy toast. The restaurant's so old it's still split down the middle when one side was smoking and the other non. Now it's all non, but we still divide the table service that way.

It's Tuesday. It's slow. Jared and I are covering the whole place.

"You know," he says, when we meet back at the waitress station (still called the waitress station even though it's only us two waiters tonight), "this thing with Henna only really came up when she started dating Tony. And now she's going to Africa after graduation. And then *Nathan* comes into our lives to catch her eye when she's single and you're still 'gathering your courage'." He eats a french fry off a plate. "Ever thought you only really like her because there's always something in the way of actually getting close to her?"

"I think that all the time."

"Seven wants more raspberry lemonades," Tina, our manager, says, looming into the waitress station. She sets down the two pots of coffee she's used on her refill run and takes a slice of cheesy toast off one of my plates. "I swear they put crack in these," she says, eating it.

I deliver my plates, I get three more raspberry lemonades for table seven, I bring enough extra cheesy toast into the restaurant to feed the entire population that has ever lived on this planet. Grillers is high volume, fast turnover, and even if the tips are cheap, there are a lot of them. It's a great job. It keeps gas in my car. It gets me out of the house. I work a lot of shifts with Jared. I'm lucky, too: Mel works the tills at a twenty-four-hour drugstore, fighting off meth heads who've lost track of what year it is, and Henna makes coffee at a drive-in Java Shack that doesn't even have its own bathroom.

It's a great job. I'm lucky. It's a great job.

(But do you have any idea how dirty restaurants are?)

I start washing my hands early in the shift, and five hours later at the end, I'm washing them almost every two minutes, which by then doesn't feel like often enough after touching one of the sponges we use to wipe the crevices of the booths after we close.

"One hundred and thirty-five." Jared counts his money, sitting on the steps down from the storeroom. "One hundred and thirty-six dollars and ... seventy-two cents." He straightens all the bills into a neatish pile and shoves them into his polyester uniform pocket. "Not bad for a Tuesday." He looks over to where I'm standing at the prep room sink. "What about you?"

"A hundred and seventeen even," I say, rinsing off the soap. I leave the water running. I've washed my hands so many times tonight two of the fingertip pads on my right hand have cracked and started bleeding. The skin from my fingers to my wrists itches and burns because I've washed every bit of natural oil out of it. I grip my hands into fists, bearing the pain.

Then I squirt some more soap on them and start washing them again.

"You guys are the lucky ones," Tina says. She's in the closet-sized office they give to the managers. The door is open, and she's basically sitting next to Jared, her cheek resting on her computer keyboard, volumes of blonde hair splayed out over the desk. "You're so young. You're so lucky and *young.*"

"You're only twenty-eight," Jared says.

"I *know*," Tina moans.

Jared gives me a quizzical glance as I wash my hands again. "Tell your Uncle Jared what's wrong this time, Tina."

She shoots him a dirty look, her face still moulded

onto the keyboard. But she answers anyway. "I think Ronald's cheating on me."

"With *who*?" Jared's a little too surprised.

"Hey!" Tina says. "Ronald's an attractive guy!" She hesitates. "A little *short*, but..."

Ronald, who stops by every Saturday afternoon for a free lunch, comes up to Tina's shoulders. And Jared's belt.

I'm only slightly exaggerating.

"Is it revenge for your thing with Harvey the Chef?" Jared asks.

Tina sits up, a cluster of keyboard squares embossed on her cheek. "Probably."

I squeeze another blob of soap on my hands. I can feel my chest start to constrict, actual tears welling up in my eyes. I'm just *burning* with rage at myself.

But I rinse off the soap and start again.

"He'll come back," Jared says, standing. "He always does. So do you."

"He hasn't *gone* anywhere," Tina says, locking the safe and picking up her purse. "That's kind of the problem. If he left, I'd at least be able to clean up the house a little before he came back." She flicks off the light in the office. "You know he actually once lost a whole frozen turkey? And not even in the kitchen."

"Mm-hmm," Jared says, his eyes on me.

"You guys done?" Tina asks, locking the office door.

"Almost," I say, hoping she doesn't hear the crack in my voice.

She doesn't. "Good. I'm going to go set the alarm and then we're outta here." She heads out into the main restaurant where the alarm pad is, disappearing past the walk-in freezer.

In two steps, Jared is behind me, putting his bigger, longer, stronger arms around me to pin my own against my side. He turns it into a kind of imprisoning bear hug, lifting me up and away from the sink. He just holds me there for a second, a few inches off the ground, neither of us saying anything. His forehead's against the back of my head and I can feel his breathing on my neck. I'm not exactly a small guy, but I'm thin and a bit wiry, while Jared is enormous, tall and broad and just big, big, big.

Thank God he's not a bully or he'd terrorize the school.

"Okay?" he asks quietly, after a minute.

"Okay," I whisper, swallowing the huge lump in my throat.

He sets me down and slowly, gently, in the way that he has, he lets me go. I don't move. He steps around me, turns off the tap and hands me some paper towels. I wince as I grab them, leaving several drops of blood against the white.

Tina yawns her way back to us. She scratches a spot on her scalp with one long fake fingernail. "I wonder what Harvey the Chef is up to these days?" she says.

Jared keeps looking over at me as he drives us home. He's got a ridiculously tiny (and old) car for such a big guy, but it's just him and his dad and they aren't overflowing with money.

They're happy, though. His dad's the nicest grown man I've ever met.

"It really *has* gotten bad again," Jared says, a statement rather than a question, as we drive deeper into the dark woods towards our homes.

"I know," I say. "I've been getting stuck in these kind of … *loops* lately and it's getting harder and harder to get out of them."

"Even when it's hurting you?"

"Even when I know it's stupid. In fact, knowing it's stupid, knowing that I've already washed my hands a hundred goddamned times, actually makes it worse. Because knowing that and doing it anyway is like…"

I don't finish. We drive in silence for a little longer.

"Your fucking parents, man," Jared whispers. He raises his voice. "If you ever need a place, Mikey. I don't care how mad they get or how it affects her stupid career–"

"Thanks."

"I mean it."

"I know."

He hits the steering wheel with his fists. I feel kind of shy about how upset he is on my behalf.

But that's Jared for you.

"Four and a half weeks," he says.

CHAPTER THE FOURTH, *in which Satchel and Dylan sit in a coffee house with understated live music and discuss what Satchel's uncle told them; Dylan also tells her it's clear that second indie kid Finn has feelings for her; Satchel doesn't see that this is Dylan's way of saying that he has feelings for her, too; later, the Messenger of the Immortals makes a surprising offer to indie kid Kerouac.*

◄o►

Okay, look, I gotta get some stuff out of the way. I wish I didn't, but it's necessary. This doesn't define me or any of the people I love, okay? It's just life. And we've moved on.

But you gotta know.

So.

Four years ago, when I was thirteen and she was

still fourteen, my sister had a heart attack. It was caused by arrhythmia, which was caused by Mel starving herself to death.

In the ambulance on the way to the hospital, she died. They were able to revive her, obviously, but the fact remains that, for three or four minutes, she was gone, we'd lost her. She says she doesn't remember anything about it: no lights, no tunnels, no angels or old relatives or prickly-faced Labradors to help her with her journey to the other side. But weirdly, she doesn't remember the opposite either. She doesn't remember nothingness or emptiness or oblivion. Her memory stops before the heart attack and picks up again in the hospital.

"Don't you wish you could remember?" I once asked her.

She looked at me as if I'd suggested murdering a duckling. "Absolutely not."

Where were we at this point as a family? Mom was in the Washington State Senate and was running for Lieutenant Governor. I'm going to guess that your knowledge of/interest in state and local politics is as non-existent as most people's, but it's enough to know that this was something she considered both extremely modest and a big, big deal. She'd planned it for almost three years, *way* more than the other candidates seemed to, and we'd been photographed a lot in the run-up to the Primary to see if she'd be selected as her party's candidate.

Because weren't we all perfect and adorable? Weren't the Mitchells exactly what the state needed? Look at us with our healthy and unthreateningly average smiles. Our hair that spoke of middle-class prosperity but wasn't (too) much better than yours. The modern political husband, super-supportive and perhaps a bonus extra behind the scenes. The two older children with their polite attitudes and good grades, and beautiful little Meredith, precocious and funny as a later Disney heroine. Wouldn't Lieutenant Governor Alice Mitchell be your friend as well as your humble public servant while hanging around in case the Governor died?

The problem was that hardly anyone had heard of her, the campaign had no money, and polls had her at a steady but distant fourth in the Primary.

It wasn't my mom who told Mel she was looking

"a little fat" in some of the press photos; it was her one-day-a-month campaign advisor, a chain-smoking beard called Malcolm. But Malcolm did say it, and my mom didn't fire him.

Was that enough to make Mel stop eating? Maybe. But we were hardly a hotbed of mental health before then. We didn't have nearly as much money as it looked like we had, for one thing, because my dad was still paying back the thousands he embezzled from my Uncle Rick's car dealership, where he used to be top sales manager. My dad stole, under Rick's nose, all the money to buy the house we still live in. He should have been arrested. He should still be in jail.

But Rick is my mother's brother and this was even earlier in her career, when she was trying to move up from the State House of Representatives to the State Senate. A scandal would have ended her political career, so she and my dad not only stayed married, but she somehow convinced Rick to keep it secret and – if you can believe this – actually let my dad stay employed there. No access to any accounts, of course, but still selling cars until he's paid back all the money, plus interest. Which will probably take him up to retirement. As I said, Uncle Rick doesn't come around much any more.

So pretty much every day back then we were about an hour away from losing everything: money, careers, house, a father, all the while pretending we were the highly functioning family of an up-and-coming politician. My dad drank every day (always did, still does). My mom threw herself into politicking, and Mikey Mitchell – your humble narrator – was so tense I'd started to get trapped in compulsive loops for the first time. Counting and re-counting (and re-counting and re-counting) the contents of my sixth-grade arts cabinet. Driving our poor dog Martha crazy (pre-porcupine death) by walking her over the same length of road four dozen times because I couldn't seem to get it exactly "right", though I could never have told you what "right" was. I was sent to a psychiatrist called Dr Luther and was put on medication. And this was all before my mom decided to up the stakes by running for a bigger job.

So all I'm saying is that the ground was clearly fertile for craziness to grow. My sister just got stuck with one that was particularly shit.

One that killed her.

Killed my mom's campaign, too. Malcolm tried to keep the press to a minimum (and this was at the start of the vampire romances, so there were plenty of "mysterious" deaths among the indie kids to be writing about anyway), but enough got out that my mother was forced to withdraw to support her daughter through a "crisis that could hit *any* family".

We all started this thing called FBT, family-based treatment, where we were supposed to show ourselves as resources for Mel, instead of the cause of the problem. And for a time, we did. Mom set up a gradual eating routine that Mel, eventually, accepted. Me and Meredith were instructed on how to refer to food and Mel's condition in non-judgemental terms, which we were happy to do. We were so freaked out by maybe losing her we would have burnt all our clothes in a bonfire if it would have helped. Dad drank a bit less.

And Mel got better. She gained some weight, not a lot, but an amount that made her healthy again. It took a while, over a year, which is why we're both seniors now instead of her already graduating, but she braved it out and nobody gave her much shit when she went back to school. That's when she and Henna got so close, now that we were all in the same year. Meanwhile, my mom went back to the State Senate. Someone else won the Primary for Lieutenant Governor and was subsequently slaughtered in the general election by the incumbent, so my mom started calling it a "blessing in disguise" with a hard, faraway look in her eye. I finished my own counselling with Dr Luther. I stopped the anxiety medication. Things got kind of back to normal again.

And that, I think, was the problem. They could absolutely deal with Mel getting so sick. But I don't think they could quite deal with her getting better. I did about eight hundred hours of anxious research on the internet and tried to tell them that almost ninety per cent of anorexics do recover, but as time passed, they seemed to start resenting the healthy daughter just sitting there, the one that they'd sacrificed so much for, no longer needing the sacrifice, if she'd ever *really* needed it in the first place. (She did. We could have lost her. *I* could have lost her. And then what?)

My mom started making vague references to "missed opportunities" and stopped coming to FBT sessions because she was doing important work down in Olympia, the capital. She handed control of Mel's diet over to Mel four full months before the schedule suggested. Mel asked if I would help her, and I have, every day since.

We went back to barely seeing my dad. He's either in his office at work or his office at home, usually smelling of alcohol, often asleep. To be fair, as alcoholics go, he's pretty low-maintenance. He gets to work most of the time, he's never violent or scary, and he lets my mom do most of the driving. I think she keeps him out of trouble, mostly by being clear about what she would do if he were ever *in* trouble.

So here we are now. I make sure my sister eats, she helps me out of my tics and loops, and we both watch over Meredith and try to stay out of our parents' way.

But this, all this, isn't the story I'm trying to tell. This is all past. This is the part of your life where it gets taken over by other people's stories and there's nothing you can do about it except hold on tight and hope you're still alive at the end to take up your own story again. So that's what we did. Me, Mel and Meredith all moved on, and we're the stories we're living now.

Aren't we?

"It's on the twenty-fourth," Meredith says, staring at us like she's trying to light us on fire with her mind. Which maybe she is. "So three weeks from today. Aren't you going to write it down?"

"Eight hundredth time you've said it," Mel yawns, leaning back into our couch. "It's in my phone, on the calendar in my room, on TV every five seconds, and I have a feeling you'll probably remind us as the day approaches."

"It's the week before your prom so it won't get in the way and there's enough time for you to get off work–"

I grab Meredith's fingers where she's counting off her points. "It doesn't matter if we're free, the concert's gonna sell out in like two seconds."

Meredith opens up her computer pad and reads.

"'As a thank you to their local fans for this special show, Bolts of Fire have made tickets available for purchase to *any* fan'" – she looks up at us – "'between the ages of eight and twelve living in the 98--- zip code.'" She closes the pad. "You just have to be one of the first to register."

"Let me guess," I say.

"Done and dusted," Meredith says, copying a phrase from our dad. "They let fan-club members in there first."

"Now all you have to do is talk her into letting you go," Mel says.

"I *will*," Meredith says, "with your help. But you *know* she won't take me, so you guys have to be ready."

Our mom started avoiding large public gatherings she couldn't leave several years ago because they just turned into abuse-fests by people who hated politicians in general and politicians who supported a non-lethal speed limit in particular. Thirty minutes anywhere, even church, is her maximum, and on this one, I have to say I can kind of see her point.

"I'm in," Mel says. "Even though I hate country music. I'm the best sister in the world."

"I'm in, too," I say, "though as your brother, I'm probably only the second-best sister."

"But," Mel says and raises her eyebrows. She doesn't need to explain further.

Mom's aversion to public events aside, Bolts of Fire have toured near us twice before, both times in the even bigger city that's an hour away from the city that's an hour away from us. Meredith tried to beg, bribe, tantrum, reason, sweet-talk, extort, demand, and panic my mother into letting her go. But after Mel's rough time and my thing with the loops, Mom isn't taking any chances on her last remaining possibly non-messed-up child. Meredith was too young for the "atmosphere" of a rock concert (which is stretching it, as far as Bolts of Fire are concerned; they're so meticulously clean and goody-goody, the bars at the venues only serve orange Kool-Aid) and she was too young to stay up that late anyway. So no, no, end of discussion, no, don't make me take away your internet privileges.

"But I'm ten now," Meredith says. "Double digits. And it's like five minutes away. And I'll be home before my bedtime because they're having the concert early so the cancer girl can have her treatment the next morning."

Mel shrugs. "Not up to us."

"I'll die if I can't go. I'll just die. For real."

"You could tell them you have cancer, too?" Mel suggests. "That'd get you in with or without Mom."

Meredith's eyes go wide, first in shock, then with a glorious, glorious plan—

"No way, Merde Breath," I say. "For so many reasons."

A door on the upstairs landing opens. Our father comes out in his underwear. Meredith looks away. He stares down at us like he's not sure we're there. He scratches the hairy potbelly sticking out over the elastic of his briefs and smacks his lips like he just woke up. It's six o'clock in the evening, so that's a possibility.

"You guys seen that shirt of mine?" he asks, his tongue lazy with drink. "The one with the eels?"

I turn to Mel. "The eels?" I mouth.

"I think Mom's washing it," Mel lies to him. "Why don't you wear that red one with the double cuffs?"

He waits for a minute, like he didn't hear her,

then farts loudly and turns without a word back into his office.

When he's sober, our dad is a funny, smart, warm guy, criminal greed aside. Mel in particular loves him, always has since I can remember. And she's so disappointed in him, it almost literally chokes her.

Look, some more stuff happens that evening – Meredith argues with our mom over Bolts of Fire, Mel sneaks out to Henna's house – but nothing so important that I have to go on about it. Just remember, please, most of that stuff is in the past. It isn't the story I want to tell. At all.

You needed to know it, but for the rest of this, I'm choosing my own story.

Because if you can't do that, you might as well just give up.

CHAPTER THE FIFTH, *in which indie kid Kerouac opens the Gate of the Immortals, allowing the Royal Family and its Court a fissure through which to temporarily enter this world; then Kerouac discovers that the Messenger lied to him; he dies, alone.*

◄O►

On Friday, Henna and I somehow get a whole half-hour in her car alone together while she drives us back from the shop where she's getting her prom dress (custard and burgundy, apparently) and I'm renting my tux (black).

We're not going together. Well, we are, but not like that. Henna broke up with Tony after he'd already asked her to prom so anyone else she might have wanted to go with had already got other dates. Mel is a year older than everyone in our senior class and the guys who tend to ask her out are the creepy ones who think they can smell damage, in whom she has zero interest, thank God. Pretty much everyone would be totally fine if Jared brought a guy as his date, but he just gave his usual close-lipped refusal to even talk about it. As for me? I waited so long to ask Vanessa Wright, my ex-girlfriend, that she picked up the pieces of Tony Kim instead.

So guess what? Me, my sister, my best friend, and Henna are going to prom as a foursome, that ridiculous idea that only happens in the stupidest teen movies or drippiest teen books. Trust me, it only ever sounds cool if you never have to do it.

Oh, well. At least I like the people I'm going with and we'll all be in it together.

"Mike?" Henna asks as we drive.

"Yeah?"

She doesn't answer immediately. In fact, the silence goes on so long I look up from the text I'm writing to Mel to ask if she confirmed the limo we're all taking to prom. (What do you want from us? We're suburban. We *live* for shit like limos.)

"Henna?"

She sighs out through her nose. "Would you guys be really pissed off at me if I didn't go in our foursome to prom?"

Oh. Hell, no. No, no, no.

"Of course we'd be pissed off," I say. "That's why you're asking me and not Mel or Jared. I'm the one least likely to yell at you."

"Please don't yell at me," she says, turning off the main road to the wooded ones that lead to our houses. The sun has abandoned us for the past couple days, and Henna flicks on the wipers as rain starts to fall.

"Who do you want to–" I start, but there's no need to ask, is there?

"He's new," Henna says. "He doesn't know anybody and how hard must it be to come to a new school right before graduation–?"

"Henna–"

"I haven't asked him yet. But I want to." She glances over at me. "Would that be awful of me? Would you hate me for it?"

"We've arranged everything, though. It was going to be lame but at least it was going to be lame for the four of us–"

"Well, how about this? How about if it's the *five* of us?"

"But he'd be your date."

"Well. Yeah."

"*Henna–*"

"Please don't shout," she winces. "It makes my stomach hurt."

"I didn't even raise my voice."

"It sounded like you might."

This actually makes me angry. "When, in my entire life, have I ever shouted at you?"

"Never, I know." She breathes heavy for a minute. "My stomach hurts."

"You were worried about asking us."

"Yes."

"You're worried he might say no anyway."

"Yes."

"You're worried about your mom and dad not letting you go to prom with someone they've never met so you're going to pitch it that he'd come with all of us when really you just want him to come with you."

I see her swallow. "There's a war in the Central African Republic."

"...*What?*"

"They're still going to go, Mikey. They're going to give aid to refugees. But it's a war. An actual war. And they say we'll be in safe places but..."

I turn a little in my seat to look at her better. "That's crazy."

"And it's the stupid *prom* that's making my stomach hurt." She laughs, but it's thick in her throat. "I didn't want to let you guys down. And I have no idea where this comes from with Nathan–"

"You don't even know him–"

"I know! I've spoken to him like three times! But it's like I was telling Mel. It wells up in my stomach when I see him and it's so strong, I can barely put two words together and I'm a *smart person*, Mike!" She shakes her head. "Smart enough to know that it's probably not Nathan. It's going away, isn't it? It's school ending. It's going to the middle of a war. With my *parents*. My stomach hurts all the time and he's a distraction from that."

"...But a good one."

She nods. "I'm sorry to be saying this to you. Of all people."

I blink. "Of all people," I echo.

She looks at me again. And then once more. She clearly wants to say something, but doesn't know how. Or doesn't want to hurt me.

Of all people.

I stare at her profile as she drives, taking a turn, then another, then to the road that leads to our respective houses.

She's beautiful, and not in a stupid way. Sometimes she leaves her hair curly, sometimes she straightens it. It doesn't matter. It doesn't matter if she's got make-up on or not – though she regularly complains about how hard it is to get proper stuff for black skin out here in our little middle of nowhere.

But it doesn't matter. She's beautiful. The tiny scar on her cheek makes her more so, not less. The freckles that are pretty much the only inheritance from her father even more. The slight overbite. The terrible taste in earrings. None of it matters. Or if it matters, it's only because it makes everything else more beautiful.

And she knows I think so.

How could she not? She's smart, like she said, and

she's best friends with my sister. There's no way she could *not* know.

And she desires Nathan, not me. Her anxiety – which I understand, hooray – looked for a place of safety and it found Nathan. It didn't find me. And she knows how I'll take that information.

This should hurt my heart. It does. I can feel it. I should also be humiliated that she knows how I feel, and I do, I can feel that, too. But I look at her, and I just want to make it all okay.

So I have absolutely no idea why the hell I say, "I'm in love with you, Henna."

She smiles a bit at that, looking as surprised at the smile as I am at my words.

"Mikey," she says. "I don't think you are."

Then she screams at the deer that's jumped out of the trees and onto the road in front of us and there's no time to even brake and we hit it, taking its legs out from under it, which everyone in these parts knows is the worst thing that can happen when you hit a deer, because now six hundred pounds of panicked, dying, unstoppable deer carcass are flying right up the hood, straight at us–

This is how people die, I think, in that instant–

And Henna and I are both ducking to the middle of the seat and our heads hit together with a funny coconut sound and glass is breaking and metal is bending above us (which is so loud, *so* loud) and something hits me hard in the cheek and I hear Henna make a soft "oof" sound and her body shifts away from mine and it's only now I realize the car is still moving and I reach over her to try to steer but the steering wheel has snapped off and I feel us veering and tipping and we come to a slamming stop and the passenger's side air bag goes off so ferociously I actually feel my nose breaking.

Then it's quiet.

"Henna?" I say. *"Henna!"*

Her voice, when it comes, is deep and guttural, pain-filled. "My arm," is all she says.

I pull myself up to an almost-sitting position. Rain hits my face. The roof of Henna's car is peeled nearly all the way off. We're pushed up against the dashboard and I turn my neck (ow, ow, *ow*) to see that the deer somehow went all the way over the top of us, which is some kind of freaking miracle. Its bulk takes up the entire back seat, its neck broken, its dead weight pressing against us. The engine stopped when we drove into what I now see is a ditch, and I can hear movement all around us.

I must be in shock. Dozens of deer, *dozens* of them, are leaping out of the forest on our side of the road, crossing it, and disappearing through the treeline on the other side.

They keep coming. I've never seen anything like it. It's unreal.

"Mikey?" Henna says, her eyes wide with fear and the same shock as she sees what I'm seeing. Her left arm looks awful, twisted in a horrible way, so I take her right hand and hold it, as the impossible flood of deer spills around us like we're an island in a river.

"I'm not going to lie to you," the big Latino intern Dr "Call Me Steve" says, as he sews up my right cheek, "you're going to look pretty rough for a while."

"He hasn't taken his graduation pictures yet," Mel says, standing to the side of the gurney, arms crossed, and so comprehensively not flirting with Call Me Steve that, as flirtations go, it's working really well.

"Then you're going to have two black eyes in them, I'm afraid," Steve tells me. "I've reset your nose" – he glances at Mel with a smile – "which is turning out to be a specialty of mine" – he looks back to me – "so it should be close to its normal shape within a week or so, but I'd keep the bracing bandage on for a week more after that, otherwise you won't be able to breathe. And as for this" – he puts a rectangle of gauze over my stitches – "I think you were probably hit by an antler or hoof rather than glass. It's a raggedy tear. I did my very, very best, but you are going to have a scar, my friend."

"It'll make you look rugged," Mel says.

"Because I woke up this morning," I say, "and the one thing I realized I lacked was ruggedness."

"Your lucky day then," says Call Me Steve.

"It is," Mel says, and her face gets that angry look it always does when she's about to cry. "He could've been killed."

Dr Steve reads the vibe and starts to make his excuses. "Wait," Mel says. She tears a strip of paper off my admissions chart and writes down her phone number. She gives it to Steve. "It's all right. I'm nineteen. I should already be in college. You're good."

Steve just laughs, but he takes the number. "Go now, please," she says. "I'd like to yell at my brother for almost dying."

When we're alone, she doesn't yell. She just stands in front of me, gently gently gently not quite touching the wounds on my face. She *is* crying now, but her face is so fierce, I know she'd take my head off if I mentioned it.

"Mikey," she finally says.

"I know," I say.

She tries to gently hug me, too, but even that's too much. "Ribs!" I say, groaning. She just sits down next to me on the gurney.

It turns out that both the slight fascists and the pot farmers who live on our road are equally nice in a car accident. My phone disappeared somewhere under the dashboard and Henna was still pinned in, so I don't know who called 911. Before the ambulances and the fire truck even arrived, though, people were running out of their houses with towels – the first of them stopping for a moment in wonder to watch the last of the deer flood disappear – then they were pressing those towels against my face. A couple of other people tried to get Henna's door open to get her out in case the car caught fire. She screamed every time her arm moved, and she wouldn't let go of my hand, not even when Mr and Mrs Silvennoinen were retrieved from their house – we were like six doors away when the deer hit us. They were fantastically calm, so much so that it was only when I saw them that I realized how much pain I was in.

Someone called my house, too. My mom was picking Meredith up from Jazz & Tap, so Mel – not even bothering with our father – came roaring down the road in her own car. Me and Henna got taken away by ambulance, Mel and the Silvennoinens followed, and Henna went straight into surgery to put her arm back together.

The last thing she said before the paramedics knocked her out was, "Mike."

"I called Jared," Mel says now. "He's going to come by at midnight. The Field."

"Good," I say. "Thanks."

Her hand is next to mine on the gurney and she laces our fingers together, squeezing hard. You see how lucky I am? Knowing that people love me? So lucky. So stupidly lucky.

We hear our mom's voice before we see her. Mel lets go of my hand. My mom turns the curtained corner where we sit in the emergency room, and the first sight of her face is so worried, so terrified, that suddenly I'm six years old again and have just fallen off my bike and want her to make it better.

This lasts a full four seconds until she tries to hug me.

"Ribs!" I pretty much shriek.

"Sorry, sweetheart," she says, pulling back. I have to flinch again when she tries to touch my face. "Sorry, sorry, sorry."

"Can't you see the bandages?" Mel asks. "And the blood?"

"Yes," my mom says, "why hasn't anyone cleaned that off?"

"They did," I say. "Most of it."

Her face softens again. "How bad?"

I shrug, then I wince because shrugging really hurts. "Gash on my cheek, broken nose, most of my left ribs are cracked, sprained my ankle. Henna got the worst of it."

"I saw Mattias and Caroline on my way in," my mom says, meaning Henna's parents. "She's in surgery right now but aside from her arm and a broken collarbone, just bumps and bruises, like you."

"'Just'," I say.

"You know what I mean."

"I do. We're lucky. It was scary, though. And weird."

"You should see Henna's car," Mel says. "It's been decapitated."

"Where's Meredith?" I ask.

"Caroline's watching her for a minute in the waiting room," my mom says.

"Someone should tell Dad," Mel says.

Mom gets a look of fleeting irritation on her face, then swallows it. "I'll tell him when we get home." She looks at us in a particular way. "Listen, I know this isn't the time or the place–"

"Then why do it?" Mel says.

"Do what?"

"Whatever it is you're about to do."

Mom gets that fleeting look again. "Now that I know you're all right," she says to me.

"Well, I'm not exactly all–"

"You're going to see it on the news anyway and I want you to hear it from me first."

She stops, and for a confusing second, I think it's going to be about the weirdness with the deer, which no one has satisfactorily explained and which it would be extraordinary if my mother could do so, but hey, I'm still in shock here, and the idea lodges so firmly in my head, that when she says, "Mankiewicz died," I try to think if I know any deer named Mankiewicz.

"What?" Mel asks, warily.

"This morning," my mom says, a bit too eagerly. "Stroke. At his house in DC."

She stops again, and I can see her try not to smile, which even *she* must recognize is the wrong reaction to this news, in this place, with my nose looking like this.

Mankiewicz isn't a deer. He's our US Congressman and has been since before my mother was born. A million years old, beloved by this congressional district, and utterly unbeatable in every election.

Now dead.

"Seven days is the protocol," my mom says, now not even pretending not to smile. "Seven days out of respect and then I announce my intention to run for his seat." She lets this news sink in. We just stare at her. "The state party actually called me, they called *me* and *asked* me to run."

Her smile hardens for an instant. "And I suppose your friend's father is going to run as well, but he'll lose, like always, so it's pretty much mine for the taking." She turns to Mel. "And you're finally old enough to vote for me!"

Then my mom claps. She actually claps.

"Your mother's going to be a United States Congresswoman," she says. "In Washington, DC!"

"Your son is going to have a permanent scar down his cheek," Mel says.

"Oh," my mother says, "of course, I know, but it's in the news today and I thought you might–" She stops, gathers herself. "I've finally got my big chance. And we'll keep the family pictures to a minimum and no one will have to do anything they don't want to–"

"I should probably tell Meredith I'm not dead," I say.

Mel takes that as a cue to find Call Me Steve, who officially releases me and nods at Mel when she makes a "phone me" sign with her hand. Meredith is playing on her computer pad when we find her with Mrs Silvennoinen. She jumps up and wraps herself around my limping legs. "I am very upset," she says.

"I'm going to be okay, though," I say. "I'll have a cool scar."

"I'm still upset." Meredith eyes my mother. "So upset it would take something *really special* to make me feel better."

"Meredith–" my mother starts.

"How's Henna?" Mel asks Mrs Silvennoinen. She's as beautiful as her daughter, but also not, because Henna is open, where Mrs Silvennoinen – even as a music minister who has to rouse people on a Sunday morning – is always a bit of a closed door. Not unfriendly, just not your business.

"Nothing life-threatening," she says.

"Praise God," Mr Silvennoinen says, joining us. He's six foot nine and has unnervingly pale green eyes, which Henna didn't inherit. His voice is deep, his accent thick, and he's handsome in a way so scary it's like he's hypnotizing you with it.

He's always been nice to me, though. Stern, insistent on seeing me at church, and grinding Henna slowly down with his expectations, but nice. He puts a soft hand on my shoulder.

"We saw how you were there for her, Mike," he says.

"Thank you," Mrs Silvennoinen says, seriously.

And I remember these are people who haven't seen their son in four years.

The poor bastards.

Before I can answer them, the most horrible, painful wail I think I've ever heard brings the room to a standstill. The police lead a man making the noise through the waiting room. Their caps are off, and the man isn't arrested or injured. They're clearly taking him to someone who didn't make it.

"Isn't that someone's dad from our school?" Mel whispers to me. "One of the indie kids', I think."

We watch until he disappears down a deeper hallway, his wails still coming.

"I think I'd like to go home now, please," I say.

CHAPTER THE SIXTH, *in which Satchel finds a note on her pillow from Kerouac, a friend since childhood who always climbed the tree outside her window to sneak inside; the note tells her he thinks he's made a terrible mistake and that she should wear the amulet he's also put on her pillow, no matter what happens; Satchel puts the amulet on, then calls her police officer uncle, who has already taken Kerouac's father to identify his son's remains.*

<o>

My alarm goes off that night at 11:30 p.m. I wouldn't normally be asleep that early, but I couldn't put off taking at least half a painkiller. It turns out there are muscles you didn't even know could hurt until they're suddenly crashed into by a huge flying deer. I get up slowly, very slowly, and even then I can't keep from calling out in pain. I pull on a hoodie, but actually find it too painful to reach down and tie my shoes, so I slip into some flip-flops.

I wait and listen. The house is quiet. Mom went to bed early because she's going down to the capital in the morning for meetings with the state party about getting the jump on Mankiewicz's seat. No one else would care if I was up anyway.

Mary Magdalene greets me on the landing, staring at me intently.

"Come on, then," I whisper and she follows me down the stairs, purring already. I let myself out the front and try not to crunch too much on the gravel in the driveway. The rain's stopped but a fog has come on; the faraway streetlights down our road give the world a blank white glow. Mary Mags does a silent little cat run ahead of me, exiting out our driveway and softly on towards the entrance of the Field.

Where Jared's car is parked.

In my lifetime, we've had 1) the undead, 2) those soul-eating ghosts, 3) the vampire cycle of romance and death, and 4) whatever might be happening now with the body of Finn and the terrified deer, if they're even connected (they're probably connected). When Jared's grandad was a teenager, they had Gods.

The indie kids back then, who were probably called hipsters or something, fought and some of them died and a crack opened in the ground and ate a whole neighbourhood, but of course the Gods and Goddesses were defeated in the end because we're all still here. They were sent back to wherever they'd come from, and the world, as it always does, got on with pretending it never happened. The crack was put down to a volcanic earthquake, and history forgot.

Except for one Goddess, who had met Jared's future grandad (called Herbert, clearly not a hipster) and liked what she saw. They married. They had a daughter, Jared's mom – there's a whole story there, but Jared's even more private about this than liking guys. (Jared's secretive about everything. Jared isn't even his first name, it's his middle. His first is so totally awful, no one knows it but me.)

Anyway, Jared's half-Goddess mom married Jared's

dad and they had their son, born two months and two days before I was. His grandma and his mom aren't around any more. Grandma went back to her realms when Herbert died and his mom runs this international charity trying to save lions, tigers and leopards from extinction. I think she might still be technically married to Jared's dad, but she hasn't been around since Jared was a kid. Which just leaves Mr Shurin, who teaches junior high Geography. We had him in the eighth grade.

Jared told me he thinks of himself as "three-quarters Jewish, one-quarter God", which he also said makes him ask lots of questions he doesn't really know the answers to. He had a bar mitzvah. It was so much fun.

Mostly, though, he doesn't talk about it, the God thing, which you probably wouldn't either if your grandmother was the Goddess of Cats and you were a great big eighteen-year-old gay linebacker trying to live a normal, non-indie kid life. It might have been different if she'd been, like, Goddess of Fire or War or Prosperity or something. Still, I've known Jared my whole life and he's never once acted resentful about the way cats, well, *worship* him. He treats them kindly, patiently, he gives them recognition, and he sends them on their way.

He can also heal them.

"Now you know there are limits here, right?" he says, putting a hand on my cheek. "You're not feline and I'm only the grandson of the real deal."

"I know," I say.

"I just don't want you to get your hopes up about what I can do."

"I haven't."

"I would if I could."

I laugh a little, then wince at the ache. "That's what everyone knows about you, Jared. You *always* would if you could."

"Well," he says, "people think they know a lot of stuff. This might hurt."

There's a sudden heat on my cheek that feels like it's pulling at my stitches and light comes faintly from the palm of Jared's hand. I try not to flinch as it gets hotter, but then he stops. He peels back the bandage.

"Looks a little better," he says. "I don't think I can do anything about the scar, though."

"It's okay," I say. "It feels a *lot* better."

And it does. It's still tender to the touch, but it feels like it's three or four more days along the healing process. That's about all Jared can do to non-cats, but it sure as hell takes the ache out of my ribs when he touches them and makes my nose feel a lot less like I've got an apple-sized cold sore on my face.

He's always done this for us. Sports injuries, colds, headaches. He can't quite get rid of them, but our doctors and parents are constantly amazed at how robust our immune systems are. He also can't do anything about what's wrong *inside* our heads – what's in your head is still illness, but *way* more complicated than any muscle ache; those times he saves me from the loops, he's just saving me as a friend, rather than a God – but he's made a whole lot of other shit a whole lot easier.

But now here's the thing: you may not believe this. You may not believe *any* of this, actually – about his grandma, about Jared, hell, about the indie kids or the vampires or whatever – you may think this is all down to my own mind making my body feel better because I *believe* that Jared can. But I don't care what you think, not about these things anyway. If you don't think they're real or important or you think that we'll all grow out of this nonsense, well, that's not really my business. I can't tell you what's real for you.

But in return, you can't say what's real for me either. *I* get to choose. Not you.

Jared sits back in his seat, tired, and looks out into the fog. Mary Magdalene is sprawled in the back, purring like she's just had the best sex of her life. There are other neighbourhood cats out there, too, tons of 'em, attracted by Jared acting Godly, which I guess is like a cat lighthouse. You can see their eyes reflecting the headlights from Jared's car, and several have hopped up on the hood and trunk, all of them purring, some of them kneading their paws gently against the metal or the windows.

"I'll try to sneak in to see Henna in the morning," Jared says. "Though I'll have to avoid her mom and dad." He turns to me. "How did I get so unpopular among parents? I'm the kind of kid other parents are supposed to *love*."

Henna's parents have never said exactly why they don't like Jared, but it's easy to guess. There are rumours about Jared's parentage that even Jared can't keep from circulating, and if very religious Mr and Mrs Silvennoinen don't actually quite believe them, the stories still leave a kind of residue that makes them nervous.

For my parents – or my mom, at least – the answer's a whole lot simpler.

"You heard about Mankiewicz?" I ask him.

"Oh, yeah. Here we go again."

Mr Shurin has run against my mother in every single one of her elections. He's *lost* every single one – the political demographic out here is never going to get him more than forty-five per cent of the vote – but he keeps on running. They're in exactly the same district for *everything*, so he's been up against her for the State House the four times she ran, both times for the State Senate, and now almost certainly again for Congress.

It's occasionally made our friendship a bit strange. Well, strang*er*. But we've stuck it out, much to my mom's annoyance. Mr Shurin is so nice it'd never occur to him that we could be anything *but* friends.

"I'll bet Mel will vote for your dad," I say.

"I don't know if she should," he says. "Feels weird, doing that against your own parent."

"You can't stand my mother."

"Yeah, but there's no need for war, is there? No need to actually hurt someone."

"Thinking like that might be why your dad loses all the time."

Jared laughs. "I don't think he'd know what to do if he ever won."

"Won't be for months anyway," I say. "Not 'til we're both gone. Maybe this time we can just leave them to it."

Jared and I are going to different colleges – both of us with scholarships and huge loans that will probably follow us until death – but those colleges are in the same city, two states away. The plan is, we'll stay friends. The plan is, we'll maybe get an apartment together later to save money. The plan is, maybe we never come back to this town.

The colleges are forty-five minutes apart, though. Is it going to be as easy as I hope? To keep our plans?

Even here, we don't get into the town that's an hour away very often.

But I don't want to think about that right now.

I stretch in the passenger seat, feeling the aches lessen by quite a lot. I can even reach down to my feet, which are freezing now in the stopped car. Movement catches my eye, and I watch a mountain lion emerge from the fog and circle over to Jared's side.

"Hey there, Missus," he says, opening his car door. He puts his hand on the mountain lion's head and does one long stroke all the way down to the end of her tail. Ever heard a mountain lion purr? Like a broken drain. She leaves huge cat footprints on the damp of the field as she sits like a statue a little bit away from the car, just a dark spot in the shadows. I know from experience that she'll wait there patiently until we leave, guarding us from danger, if she can.

"Now *that*," Jared says, closing his door. "That shit's crazy."

"I told Henna I loved her," I say. "Right before we hit the deer."

He looks at me, surprised. "She have time to say anything back?"

I breathe in slowly through my nose. Then I realize I *can* breathe through my nose. I touch it lightly. "Good job," I say.

"Thanks."

"She said she didn't think I did."

Jared looks thoughtful. "That's a weird response."

"Yeah," I say.

"Yeah."

"...but I held her hand until the paramedics got there. And the last thing she said before they knocked her out was my name."

I don't tell him what she said about Nathan and the prom. I'm kind of hoping the accident will have made her forget. Is that bad?

"Dude," Jared says, rubbing his eyes, "healing kind of takes it out of me. I think I need to get to bed."

"Yeah," I say. "Thanks again."

"No problem, my friend." He takes a deep breath and opens his door again. "Let me go hand out benedictions first."

A hundred cats and one mountain lion watch him eagerly as he steps out towards them, hands up.

"How you feeling?" Mel asks, waiting for me as I come back inside.

"I think I'm lying about how okay I am with this scar."

"I thought that was a possibility."

We sit down on the couch, turning on the muted television for light. A topless woman with a gun in each hand is shooting Asian people down a long hallway. Then her cut-off jean shorts are obviously bothering her, so she takes those off and – now wearing only a G-string – keeps on shooting. I don't understand the world sometimes. Mel turns it over to a show about dogs.

"The thing about scars, though," she says. "Nothing you can do except wear them with pride."

"Says the girl with flawless skin."

"Says the girl who destroyed her tooth enamel from chronic forced vomiting. Says the girl whose boobs could be outshone by a nine-year-old boy because I starved myself through a key development stage. There's different kinds of scars, brother."

I watch the flashing, silent, nonsense images of dogs wearing costumes. "You going to be okay about Mom running for Congress?"

"Does it matter? She didn't actually ask us, did she?"

"She thinks we're all better."

"Are we? *Aren't* we?"

I repeat what I said to Jared. "It won't be for months. We'll be out of here."

Mel – who has that combination of total self-belief and utter self-doubt which is more common than people think – is planning on medical school while doubting she's going to pass History. She'll probably do both, and if her final grades are what they should be – and they will be – she's going to a college way on the whole other coast, thousands of miles away.

You shouldn't say this about your sister, but I kind of already miss her, even though she's sitting right here.

o O o

I wake up at 3:43 a.m. because my dad has sat down on my bed.

He's crying.

"I'm sorry I wasn't there," he weeps. "I'm so sorry."

He's still in his work suit. He stinks.

"Go to bed, Dad," I say. "I'm okay."

"No, you're not," he says, shaking his head. "You're not okay at all."

"All right then, I'm not okay. But it's the middle of the night and you waking me up is kind of making everything less okay by the minute."

He makes a little sobbing sound. "I should kill myself. I should just drive off a bridge and make all your lives better."

"That'd be a waste of a good car. Especially if it belonged to Uncle Rick."

"I could park the car and jump."

"What bridge, though? There aren't any around here high enough. You'd only just break your leg and then you'd be even more of a pain in the ass than you are now."

He sighs. "You're right. You're so, so right." He starts crying again.

"Dad–"

"You're a good kid, Mikey. You're the *best* kid…"
His voice breaks.

"Seriously, Dad–"

He slides to my bedroom floor, still crying. Within minutes, he's snoring.

I take my blankets and go sleep on the couch.

CHAPTER THE SEVENTH, *in which Satchel and the rest of the indie kids share their grief for Kerouac by throwing stones soulfully into a nearby lake; wandering off on her own, Satchel takes the amulet in her hand and sees a vision of the single most handsome boy she's ever seen in her life; Dylan, finding her, takes the opportunity to kiss her, and though his lips taste of honey and vegan patchouli, she pushes him away, revealing what the amulet told her; "The Immortals are here," she says.*

◄O►

I don't go to school on Monday. I'm feeling a *lot* better after Jared's healing, but I've still got a broken nose, two black eyes and an ironclad reason to stay in bed. So I take it.

My phone is still pinned in the wreckage of

Henna's car, so Mel calls me at home with the info she gathers: Jared's not in school either, maybe still recuperating from the healing and/or still trying to sneak into Henna's hospital room, which of course is where Henna still is.

"And don't freak out," Mel says. "Another indie kid is dead. Kerouac Buchanan. That's whose dad we saw in the ER."

"Shit," I say. "Kerouac was in my American Lit class."

"We're definitely into another wave of something. I hope it's not as bad as last time."

"You be careful."

"I don't think careful has much to do with it. You're the most careful person I know and you were nearly killed by a deer."

"I'm not the most careful–"

"Dad still home?"

"Nah, he sneaked off to work about eight."

"You have to admire his willpower."

"Willpower? I thought drinking too much was a lack of it."

"The opposite. Trust me. You're helpless to the

behaviour but the effort involved is just unbelievable."

After we hang up, I call Jared but his phone goes straight to voicemail and no one answers at home. That's kind of the limit of the numbers I know by heart. I wonder if I ever *will* get my phone back. Then I wonder what will happen to the poor, dead deer. Will someone eat it? Then I wonder if Henna's arm will completely heal again. Then I wonder the same about the scar on my face. Then I wonder what Henna meant when she said my name as the last thing before unconsciousness. Then I wonder what she meant by saying she didn't think I loved her.

It's occurred to me more than once to ask myself if I was gay, too, deep-down. My best friend is, after all, and we've fooled around. I wasn't exactly lying back with my eyes closed either. It was fun. I feel so safe around Jared, it seems only natural that we'd help each other let off some steam once in a while. He thinks it's because Gods, apparently, are irresistible to humans in the literal sense. Maybe. I think it's just because he's a good guy.

I'm also sure he doesn't like me that way. He said so once because he was afraid I thought that way about *him* and didn't want me to get hurt. Which I didn't and won't. So, okay, it's all a little complicated but I'd have been crazy not to at least ask myself the question.

But I dream about girls. In that way. And when I, you know, have the occasional ... intimate conversation with myself, girls again. It's what I look at online, and it's who I've dated in the past. I've had sex with two girls, too. Vanessa Wright and I lost our straight virginity together in tenth grade. We went out for a while and are still friends. And last year, I dated a girl called Darlene who was a waitress at Grillers. She was really funny and really pretty and so embarrassed when she gave me her ex-boyfriend's crabs that she actually quit her job. I would have been okay with it; a cream cleared them right up, and my mom couldn't even be all that mad because I'd otherwise been really safe. She was a bit more upset that Darlene was twenty-seven and I was sixteen, but I don't know, maybe I'm just stupid sometimes.

And then of course Henna. I've imagined us for years. Living together. Kids and homes and travel. I've imagined, you know, personal things, too, but always really respectfully. Well ... you know what I mean. You do it, too, and when *I* do, she and I are always in it together, like we're on the same team and it's us against everybody else and there's nowhere else either of us would rather be.

I imagine her as my friend.

And if I don't understand what she means about the desire in her stomach, well, so what? People are different.

I love her. I do.

Don't I?

I spend nearly an hour counting and re-counting all the different pieces of wood-panelling in the living room, then I've just got to get the hell out of the house.

The nurse – actually, I'm not sure he *is* a nurse, I'm not even sure this old people's home has nurses or doctors or what, but he's *dressed* like a nurse – leads me down the hall to my grandma's room. I don't come here very often and I think I can feel nursey judging me for that.

"Maggie?" he says, gently at first, then more loudly. *"Maggie."*

My grandma turns to look at us, no sign of recognition at all.

"Maggie, your grandson is here to see you," says the nurse.

My grandma stares at me. "Phillip?"

You'd think "Phillip" would be her dead husband or father or something, but no one has any idea who he is or was. We're not especially convinced Grandma does either.

"No, Grandma," I say. "It's Michael."

"Where've you been, Phillip?" she says, and her eyes fill with tears.

"You want me to stay?" the nurse asks me, which is nice of him.

"Nah, I'm good, thanks."

He waits another second, then leaves. My grandma shares her room with two other women. Mrs Richardson never gets any visitors, so my mom sometimes brings her flowers. Mrs Richardson never notices, just keeps talking under her breath about how she was wronged by someone called Rosalie. Over by the window is Mrs Choi, who never says a word in English though she'll wave back if you wave at her first. Not today, though. Her adult son is visiting, so she positions herself in a wheelchair with her back to him, pretending he's not there. He seems to take this as his due punishment, and they just sit there, silently, not saying a thing.

"I took them back, Phillip," my grandma says. "Put them away."

I sit down next to her bed. "Put what away, Grandma?"

"There's a…" She frowns. "Red." Then she stares off into space.

Kooky Alzheimer's in movies really pisses me off. You know, where Grandma is sweet and funny and says hilarious-but-wise things right on cue? Real Alzheimer's is nothing like that. Nothing. It's terrifying and annoying and so sad you want to kill yourself. My parents finally put Grandma in a home after she poured boiling water down her whole left side because she couldn't identify what a pot was. She burnt herself so badly she can still barely walk.

"Well, let's see," I say. "Graduation is four weeks away. I'm doing really well in my classes and I'm not too worried about finals. Most of my hard stuff was last semester anyway, and it's really only Calc and English that I'm going to have to study for–"

"Phillip?"

"Got my tux for prom. I'll bring you pictures. Though the girl I was hoping to go with is trying to back out of our stupid plan–"

"Phillip, there's–"

"Meredith seems to be wearing Mom down about this Bolts of Fire concert, so me and Mel may end up having to take her–"

"Your *nose*, Phillip."

She's staring at the bandages on my face. Both of my eyes are still black, too, and I suddenly wonder if I look too gruesome to visit, if I'm frightening her. Nursey should have said something. Maybe *that's* why he offered to stay.

"I got into a car accident, Grandma," I say, "but it's okay. I'm all right. I even drove myself here."

Which I did. Flinching at every sudden movement in the corner of my eye.

"In fact," I say, touching her arm. She looks at my hand, but doesn't pull away. "Things aren't actually too bad. I mean, you know, I still haven't gotten anywhere with Henna, but she said my *name*. Which has got to mean something. And we're graduating soon and Jared and I will be in the same city, which is cool. And Mel's looking good, healthier than ever–"

I stop her from pulling her nightgown off over her head. She takes the correction easily and even drinks from a glass of water when I offer it.

"So," I say. "What I can't figure out is, why am I so worried all the time? If I stop and look, things are okay. They could be better – there's this guy in school that Henna likes, your daughter-in-law is running for office again – but I'm almost in a new life, one I'm looking forward to, I think."

Grandma just stares at me.

"But I'm going to have a scar on my face. Everyone says it'll look cool, but how can they know? And … and I'm counting things again. I'm getting trapped. I feel like something awful is going to happen if I don't do these insane things over and over again. Actually, I feel like something awful's going to happen anyway. I feel that all the time. Even when I'm happy."

"Happy," Grandma repeats. Then she screams three times in a row, loud enough for Mrs Richardson,

Mrs Choi and her son to all turn and look. But my grandma goes silent again, confused-looking, her eyes wandering around the room, trying to find something to focus on.

"What if..." I say, quietly. "What if I *am* going crazy? What if I get trapped in a loop and there's no one to get me out?"

Grandma's eyes find mine, rest briefly, then keep wandering.

"What if I get trapped," I say, "like you are?"

"Phillip," she says, almost pleading. *"Phillip?"*

A terrible smell knocks me back. My grandma is softly weeping as I go to find the nurse.

Yeah, kooky Alzheimer's *really* pisses me off.

Henna's car is still in the ditch. I drove past it on my way to see my grandma. Someone's covered it with a tarp, but otherwise, it's just sitting there. It's Monday, so maybe they were waiting for the weekend to finish. Maybe they'll tow it away today. And that's what makes me stop on my way back from the nursing home.

I want my phone.

I park and get out. The weather's warmed up to normal May sunshine, and you can smell the deer even though it's only been a couple days. Nothing too rank yet, nothing as bad as it *will* get. We once had a possum die under the living room. You wouldn't *believe* how bad something that small can stink.

I look around. We really do live out in the boonies. There's no one, just the ends of driveways leading into thickets of trees. And why should I feel like I'm trespassing anyway? It's *my* phone.

The tarp's tied on pretty tight with a nylon rope. I walk around the wreck, trying to find a weak spot. The driver's side door wouldn't close properly after they pried it open, and the ropes are looser there. A flap of the tarp lifts right up. I duck down and look inside. The roof is sheared nearly all the way off, so it's like looking into a convertible with the top down. Covered in a tarp.

The deer smell is *much* stronger here, and the trapped heat makes it even worse. There's a kind of tunnel across the driver's seat past the broken steering wheel. I can't fit to crawl all the way in, but I think I can lean in far enough to feel around.

I start to worm my way in, breathing through my mouth, trying not to inhale hot rotting deer. My ribs ache at the tight fit, but I make it far enough to reach down to the passenger's side floor. It's not the same shape it used to be; it's shorter, rounder, no longer any places to put your feet.

"Hah!" I say, my fingertips finding my phone. I pull it out between two fingers and look at it there, still stretched across the seat. The glass on the front is cracked, but I manage to turn it on and get a few seconds of display out of it before the battery dies. At least it worked.

The smell of deer is getting worse, so I start to pull myself gently out of the car–

Which is when everything lights up. The sun is shining, but this is way more than that. Every shadow under the tarp disappears, bathed in blue. I can see the head of the deer pressing on the back of the passenger's seat. I can see the metallic eyes of the flies crawling over the deer's skin. Then the light gets even brighter, so much I actually have to squint against it.

All I can think of is the pillar of light we saw from the Field right after indie kid Finn ran past us.

Indie kid Finn who turned up dead.

I'm afraid to get out from under the tarp.

I'm afraid to *not* get out from under the tarp.

But then it stops. The light drops so fast I'm blinded for a second and have to blink to see again in the normal shadowy, tarp-covered sunlight.

I listen. It's silent.

And then it's not silent.

There's a sound. Nearby. One that wasn't there before.

Something's breathing.

It's the deer. It's the freakin' *deer*. I see its head move and a wet, disgusting snuffle of breath comes out the end of its nose.

I pretty much throw myself out of the car, tumbling back into the ditch, as the deer starts butting its short antlers against the tarp. The same antlers that scarred my cheek as the deer was flying *to its death*. It bucks and jumps, until most of the tarp slips off the back.

And there it is. Standing in Henna's car.

Its neck is obviously broken, so are its legs, but it

stands on them, seemingly without pain. It shakes the flies from its hide, and I can hear a horrible *snap* as its neck, mostly, rights itself. Then it looks down at me.

Its eyes glow blue, actually *glow*, and on my back in a soggy ditch as it stands over me, it's pretty much all I can do not to wet myself.

Then it looks past me, into the woods from where all the deer came that night. It leaps gingerly, gracefully, out of the car, over the ditch, and onto the ground. Its legs are nightmarish, no *way* they should be able to support its weight.

But they do. And with a snort, it heads off into the trees, disappearing from sight.

CHAPTER THE EIGHTH, *in which Satchel, Dylan and second indie kid Finn throw themselves into research in the library, trying to find any mention of the Immortals; later that week, at Kerouac's funeral, Satchel's parents hug her and give her space to grieve; meanwhile, the Court of the Immortals, unable to live in this world for more than brief periods, begins its search for permanent Vessels in earnest; they find Satchel's uncle, passed out in his police cruiser on a dark wooded road known for its night-time activities; "Sandra?" he says on waking, just before his head is removed from his shoulders, not entirely painlessly.*

◄O►

"But I've got German to study," Meredith says, still protesting from the back seat, holding up

PATRICK NESS

her German worksheets.

"Don't you like miniature golf?" I say.

"No one likes miniature golf," she says. "You don't like it either. You're just doing it ironically."

"Well, that's probably true. Henna can't even hold a club and it was her idea."

"I still don't see why I have to come."

She has to come because no one goes out alone any more. Ever since the zombie deer, ever since two indie kids died. Me and Jared only do shifts together at Grillers, Mel claims she needs to study for finals so gets out of all her night hours at the drugstore, and Henna's off work from the Java Shack anyway because of her arm. My mom is down at the capital more and more for her campaign, so Mel and I take over driving Meredith to her nightly lessons. And prom night (under three weeks away now, tick, tock) with all of us going together is now definitely on, Nathan included and Dr Call Me Steve a late addition, because we don't think it's safe any other way. Fun, fun, fun.

Mel glances in the rear-view mirror. "Quit complaining or we won't take you to Bolts of Fire."

"Mom hasn't said yes yet, remember?" I say, as

Mel pulls onto our little bit of freeway. "And we can still make her say no."

"She'll say yes," Meredith insists. "I've already got the tickets– Oh." She says the last like she's revealed too much. Which she has.

I turn around in my seat. "You want to say that again?"

Meredith looks panicked, and I can see her brain whirring as she tries to think of an explanation.

"*Meredith,*" Mel warns.

Meredith sighs in defeat. "I already got the tickets."

"When?" Mel asks.

"*How?*" I say.

"My credit card," Meredith says, quietly.

"Your what?" Mel asks, her voice as sharp as a paper cut. Meredith stays quiet. "Mom got you a credit card, didn't she?"

"It's not *mine*," Meredith says. "It's linked to Mom's."

"Does it have your name on it?" I ask.

"Well ... *yes*, but–"

"I don't believe this," Mel says with a harsh laugh. "That woman."

"You both have *jobs*," Meredith complains. "I had no way of buying things for myself."

"You're *ten*, Merde Breath," I say.

"Don't call me that. She got tired of always having to input the number for my online music courses."

"So she got you your own card," Mel says. "Because that's the *most logical solution* to that non-problem."

"I wasn't supposed to tell you."

"I wonder why." Mel's voice is angrily light. "God knows she treats us all equally so why would there be any problem?"

"I'm being really responsible with it."

"Bolts of Fire tickets weren't responsible," I say.

Meredith looks shifty. "She won't get the bill until after the concert."

This actually makes both Mel and me laugh out loud.

"I only had a short time for the fan-club tickets!" Meredith rushes on. "If I didn't get them then, I'd *never* have got them. Anyway, they came in the mail yesterday." She smiles like the sun rising. "Three tickets."

"Why three?" Mel asks. "You could have just got two. Cheaper. Less trouble later."

"You said you'd both take me," Meredith says. "It's more fun if we're all there together."

The simple love in the way she says this makes my heart hurt a little bit. Yeah, my parents are crappy, but you hurt either of my sisters and I will spend my life finding ways to destroy you.

"That's a pretty big gamble you're taking on Mom saying yes," Mel says, already exiting the freeway (told you it was little).

"She always says yes to me eventually," Meredith says. "I don't know why."

The mini-golf place is literally right by the freeway exit, so Mel's already pulling into the lot. She parks and says, without malice, "It's because you're the best of us, Meredith."

Meredith looks at me. "I don't think that."

"It's why you're with us tonight," I say. "We couldn't leave you home alone."

"Dad's there."

"Exactly."

"Is this because of all the strange stuff going on?"

she asks, almost as if she's afraid we'll answer.

Mel and I exchange a glance and decide silently in about half a second that we're not going to lie to her. "Yeah," I say. "All the strange stuff."

Meredith nods, seriously. "I thought so."

We get out of the car. I see Henna waving to us with her good hand from the little hut where you get your putters. She's with–

"Jared's here!" Meredith says, happily. "But who's that?"

And I say, "That's Nathan."

I only make it to the first hole, where I discover that, even a week after the accident, the slight torso twist to make a putt in mini-golf is too much for a still-aching muscle in my back. Jared surreptitiously heals it while Mel and Nathan take their turns.

"Sore?" Henna asks from a bench next to Meredith, who's practising her German conjugations.

"It's mostly better," I say, sitting down next to her, gingerly. "Every once in a while I get surprised by something I didn't know was hurting."

"Me, too," she says, running her fingers along her cast. "Jared helped."

Jared has rejoined Mel and Nathan at the first hole, which is decorated with little plastic dinosaurs. Mel takes her putt, then thrusts two fists in the air. "Hole in one!" she shouts. Mel is ridiculously ace at mini-golf.

"I'm surprised your parents let you come out," I say to Henna.

"And you would be right in your surprise," she says.

"*Ich schreibe, du schreibst, er schreibt–*" Meredith whispers next to us.

"But nearly dying seems to have made a whole bunch of things clearer," Henna says. "Don't you think?"

"Not really, if I'm honest."

"It has for me."

Jared and Nathan and Mel are all laughing at Nathan's inability to get the ball in the hole. "You're supposed to give up at seven strokes," we hear Jared say.

"I told my parents I was going out to see you guys," Henna says. "They didn't want me to, but I didn't ask permission. Amazing the difference it makes. Being firm. Being clear."

"Your mom and dad are right to be worried, though. Two kids are dead. They probably won't be the last."

Meredith pauses for a moment, then goes back to conjugating. *"Ich möchte, sie möchten–"*

"That's actually the reason I gave," Henna says. "I could have died. *We* could have died in that car accident. But we didn't. I could die at home just as easily as I could die out with my friends. Or, you know, in the Central African Republic."

"Ah."

"Yeah. 'Ah'."

She's looking right at me. I don't know what her eyes mean.

"I don't feel any clearer," I'm surprised to hear myself saying. "I just feel like my body is in all these different pieces and even though it *looks* like I'm all put together, the pieces are really just floating there and if I fall down too hard, I'll fly apart."

"Like a fontanelle," Henna says.

"A what?"

"The soft spot on top of a baby's head." She taps the spot on her own head. "Babies' skulls aren't fused together when they're born, otherwise they're too big to get out of the mother. They've got this spot called a fontanelle that's just kind of unprotected until the hardness grows in."

"That makes sense," I say. "I'm just one big fontanelle."

Henna laughs lightly. Then she takes my hand in hers and holds it. "Mikey," she says, but not like she's about to say anything more, just like she's identifying me, making a place for me here that's mine to exist in. I want her so much, my heart feels heavy, like I'm grieving. Is this what they meant about that stomach feeling? They didn't say it felt this sad.

The mini-golf park is old and really narrow, so even though Jared, Mel and Nathan are already on hole number three, they're still pretty much just right there, laughing, looking over to where we sit. Especially Nathan.

"*Ich esse, wir essen.*" Meredith looks up. "I'm hungry."

"Just what I was thinking," Nathan calls. Henna

lets go of my hand. "Anyone want any food?" Nathan asks, coming over.

"A hot dog," Meredith says.

Nathan raises his eyebrows.

"A hot dog, *please*," Meredith says.

"I'll help you," Henna says, getting up. She looks back to me. "You want anything, Mikey?"

"*Ich liebe,*" Meredith mutters under her breath, "*du liebst–*"

I aim a sideways kick at her. "Nah, I'm good."

I watch them head back to the hut which sells your standard mini-golf food: hot dogs and nachos. I watch Henna go inside with Nathan. Jared's watching, too, then he looks at me and I know what he's thinking. He's thinking it's long past time I gave Henna up.

And maybe he's right.

But she held my hand again. And said she was seeing things more clearly.

I wish I was.

"Two!" Mel shouts, triumphantly.

oOo

Midway through our second round of mini-golf –
Mel won the first with a score of fifty-nine; Jared had
eighty, Nathan ninety-seven, which was pleasing –
we have a surprise visitor.

"Hey," a tired-looking Dr Call Me Steve says,
holding his car keys, still wearing hospital scrubs.

"Hey," Mel says, every word of her body language
turning into a smile. "You came."

"Who could say no to putt-putt golf?"

"Almost anybody," Meredith says, writing down
answers about the adventures of Dieter and Frederika
in Hamburg.

"Can I play in?" Steve asks, after Mel introduces
him around. ("Wow," he said, gently palpating my
nose. "That's healing amazingly fast.")

"You can have my spot," Nathan says. "I'm doing
so bad you'll be lucky to break a hundred."

Steve takes Nathan's putter. "I like a challenge."

We're on the new course at the back of the mini-
golf place, though it's only new like New Mexico is
new. It used to be jungle-themed but the statues of
"natives" were so racist they all had to be removed.
Now it's just leafy with one chipped-paint, fibreglass

tiger in the middle, emitting a tinny, pre-recorded roar every four minutes.

Henna immediately joined Mel at the arrival of Dr Steve – for moral support, I guess – so Meredith and I get Nathan all to ourselves on the bench. Yippee.

"How you feeling, Mike?" he says, sitting down between us.

"Oh, you know," I say, not meeting his eye. "Just the physical and emotional fallout of a near-death experience. Nothing big."

He laughs. Which I find irritating. "I know," he says. Which I find even more irritating.

I get up. "Anyone want any more food?"

"*Nein,*" Meredith says, crunching a nacho. "*Ich habe viele Nachos.*"

"You don't like me," Nathan says, and I stop.

"Who says I don't like you?"

"Every single vibe coming off you. Unless I'm wrong?"

I hesitate – not on purpose – just long enough to make it awkward.

"I suppose I kind of get it," he says. "You're already ninety per cent out of here, aren't you?

All you want to do now is spend the last weeks as close to your friends as possible because you don't want to think about leaving them behind when you go. But here comes this *interloper*, breaking up your tight-knit group right at the time you want it the most."

"Well," I say. "Yeah."

He looks at his hands, flexing them and unflexing them. "When we lived in Florida, my sister was a full-on indie kid, so I became kind of a mascot to them. The little one" – he glances at Meredith – "who tagged along and said funny things." He looks at his hands again. "And then the vampires came. My sister fell in love. Before it was all over, she and every one of her friends were dead."

"Oh, no," Meredith says, wide-eyed.

"My mom's been moving around from base to base ever since. Keeping busy so she never has to think about it. But we show up here and now there's two dead kids and I don't know anyone…"

"Yeah," I say. "Yeah, all right." We're quiet for a second, then I say, "You know, Henna's older brother–"

"I know," he says. "Cool to talk to someone who knows what it's like."

Shit. I mean, *come on*. How am I supposed to react to all of this? How am I supposed to hate him *now*?

"You have a really stupid haircut," I say.

"I'm self-conscious about my ears," he says.

There's a burst of laughter from the golfers and we look up to see Mel pulling a sheepish Dr Steve out of the six-inch-deep water trap.

"We good?" Nathan asks.

"Oh, God," I groan. "We were until you said 'We good?'."

Mel and Dr Steve head off to a late dinner together, so I take her car to drive Meredith home. Jared drives himself, and Nathan gives Henna a lift. Before they go, Henna hugs me.

"Clear doesn't mean I know what to do," she says, so only I can hear it. "It's just that the accident made it clear how important you are to me, Mikey. How much I love you."

"Just not in your stomach," I try to smile.

She doesn't say anything for a second, then, "You working Sunday?"

"No," I say. "Getting graduation pictures in the afternoon. I'll be under about five inches of make-up."

"Pick me up after," she says. "I'll skip evening church. Let's do something. Just the two of us."

"Okay."

"Okay?"

"Okay."

And then she leaves. With Nathan.

Meredith falls asleep singing "Bold Sapphire" while we're driving home. She wakes up once and says, "I wish you and Mel weren't going away." Then she curls into herself and goes back to sleep.

CHAPTER THE NINTH, *in which Satchel visits the police station looking for her uncle; the other officers are stern with her and she sees a glowing blue deep in their eyes; her uncle – wearing a scarf despite the heat of the day – has the same glow; he threatens Satchel, and she flees the police station, finding second indie kid Finn at her house; for a moment it seems like he might kiss her, but she touches the amulet and sees another flash of the handsomest boy she's ever seen; it's so strong, she has to run up to her room so she can ruminate alone.*

"Did you ask him yet?"

"It's not really that simple," Jared says. "And he's not really a he. You look like you're being treated for burns."

I touch the make-up the photographer has slapped on me like frosting on a cake. My fingertips come away peach.

"Don't touch it!" she yells from where she's setting up the camera.

"Maybe I should just go with the black eyes," I tell Jared.

"At least the bandages are off," he says.

"Yeah, thanks. So did you ask him? Or her? Or them?"

"It's a bit less certain than that with some Gods. But yes, I asked the God of Deer about your deer zombie."

"And?"

"Nothing. Hadn't heard about it, looked into it, said, *Beyond my realms.*"

"What does that mean?"

"It means whatever this is, it's nothing to do with the Gods." He squints and rubs his nose. No make-up for him. "Look, Mike, most Gods don't care."

"About what?"

"About anything. Other than gaining dominance over other Gods and telling you how wonderful they are and demanding that you say the same." There's some feeling in his voice when he says it. "There's nothing like a bunch of Gods to show you how alone you really are."

"Dude," I say. "I'm sitting right here. You're not alone."

"You're up!" the photographer says to me. "And make it quick. That stuff's gonna turn into a lava flow under these lights."

"Wow, that's a lot of make-up," Mr Shurin says when we stop by Jared's house after the photos are done.

"Hi, Mr Shurin," I say.

"You look like a TV anchorman."

Jared and Mr Shurin hug in greeting. They always have, even now, when Jared is basically a giant over his father. He's a good guy, Mr Shurin. Even short and kinda soft, you can still see why a half-Goddess might enjoy his company.

"I'm afraid it's officially going to be me against your mom again, Mike," he says. "The state party even hired me a proper campaign team." He shrugs. "That'll be new."

"We'll be two states away," I say. "So good luck. Text me the result or something."

He smiles, but he looks tired. There's no way he's going to win and he knows it, but the opposition party have to put up *somebody*. Mr Shurin's never said exactly why he always runs, but my guess would be that my mom's party tend to not be so thrilled with people who are different. There's a *lot* of different in Mr Shurin's life.

It looks like it might be wearing on him though. He's got more grey hair on his temples than even last month. It's never really occurred to me to wonder how me and Mel moving out will affect my parents because realistically the answer's got to be: not that much. But Jared's an only child, he's really close to his dad, and his mom isn't around any more. Funny how you can forget that every family isn't like yours.

I really want to go and wash off my face, but Mr Shurin sticks a Coke in my hand and pulls a pizza he's obviously had waiting for us out of the oven. We sit and eat, flakes of make-up falling onto my pepperoni.

"Jared asked you about the cabin?" Mr Shurin says.

I look up, chewing cheese. "What?"

"After prom."

"Dad wants us to throw a party out there," Jared says. "When we're done dancing."

"Not a party," Mr Shurin says. "The *prom's* a party. This would be an after-party. A chill-out."

Jared winces at his dad's ancient slang.

"Look," Mr Shurin says, "I *know* you guys are going to drink and hang out somewhere, so why not do it in a safe place no one has to drive home from?"

The cabin he's talking about is a decent-sized if cheaply made shack out on the far – meaning poor – end of the big glacial lake. To call it basic would be an optimistic use of "basic", but I've been a bunch of times with them in the summer over the years and it's fine. They had a bit of an otter problem not too long ago, but the musk and rotting fish smell must have faded by now.

"Sounds fun to me," I say. "Aside from it being exactly the sort of situation where we'll all be murdered by a skin-eating serial killer or something."

Jared barely responds. He's been pre-occupied since at least this morning–

Actually, it's been longer than that, hasn't it? Now that I think about it. Now that I think about something other than myself. Oh, damn. Have I missed something? Am I letting my best friend down somehow?

"Well, it's there, the idea," Mr Shurin says. "If you want it." He takes a bite of pizza. "You boys doing anything tonight?"

He means together. I shake my head. "I'm meeting Henna."

Mr Shurin brightens. "A date? At last?"

Yes. Everyone knows. Everyone.

"I don't think so," I say. "More a car crash survivor's meeting."

Mr Shurin nods, then looks at Jared. "You going out?"

"Mm," says Jared, wiping his mouth on a napkin. He stands and opens the back door where we came in. A dozen neighbourhood cats sit outside, patiently. "Give me a minute," Jared says.

It's the third time through washing my face that I know I'm screwed.

I'm in Jared's bathroom, and I wash in a particular order, of course, being me. I splash water on myself from the sink and rub some of Jared's medium-fancy face soap into my forehead, upper corners first with both hands, then circles to the centre. I move down my nose, washing either side, four, five, six times, out across my cheekbones, my hands working in mirror, then my cheeks – gently on the still-healing scar – and across my chin with my right hand. Both hands wash under my neck, dripping water on the collar of my T-shirt. Rinse with one, two, three splashes of water, then a towel in the same pattern to dry it.

The first time I do it, whole slabs of make-up come off – I'm going to look like an Easter Island head in my senior pictures – so I wash again in the same exact order. Third time through, I know I'm gone. Forehead, nose, cheekbones, chin, neck. Forehead, nose, cheekbones, chin, neck. Forehead, nose, cheekbones, chin, neck. Shit shit shit shit shit.

My shirt is soaking wet now. I can feel my fingertips starting to crack again as the oil is washed away. The repeated washing of my black eyes and cheek scar, no matter how gently I do it, gets more painful each time.

The eighth time through, I try to force my hands to rest on the sink and fail.

I know how crazy this is. I know the feeling that I haven't washed my face "right" makes no sense. But like I said, knowing doesn't make it better. It makes it so much worse. How can I explain it? If you don't know, maybe I can't, but as I wash my face yet again, I hate myself so much I want to stick a knife in my heart.

When Jared finally opens the bathroom door to see what's going on, I'm actually crying. With fury. With embarrassment. With hate for myself and this stupid thing *I can't stop doing*. I'm doing it again even now, knowing all of those things.

Jared takes one look, disappears for a sec and returns with a dry shirt, one of mine I've left here over the years.

The simple act of taking it from him breaks the loop.

I bend forward at the waist and say a long, angry "fuuuuuuuuuuuuuck" under my breath. I'm still crying, so Jared just puts his hand on my back until I'm ready to stand up again.

"There's no shame in therapy, Mike," he says, as I change shirts. "Or medicine. You shouldn't have to go through this."

The skin on my face is now so dry it stings. Jared fishes out some man moisturizer and holds it out to me. "Can you do it?" I say. "I'm afraid I'll get stuck again."

He doesn't question me, just starts dabbing the goop on my face. "Is it going out with Henna tonight? You're afraid it's changing. That could be it."

"Maybe." I wince as the cream bites a bit. "Maybe it's you."

He pauses. "Me?"

I try to smile. "Who's going to save me from these when I go to college?"

"You'll work it out, Mikey. You're stronger than you think, and I'll be there anyway."

"It's not just that. Where've you been lately, Jared? Where do you go on Saturday nights? What are you doing *tonight* that no one can know about?"

He puts more stuff on my face. And yeah, I know most people would think it weird that two guy friends touch as much as we do, but when you choose your family, you get to choose how it is between you, too. This is how we work. I hope you get to choose your family and I hope it means as much to you as mine does to me.

"I got some stuff going on, Mike," he says.

"What stuff? I can help you with it."

He smiles. "Not this stuff. But thank you."

"You could talk to me about it. You can talk to me about anything."

"I know." He finishes with the moisturizer. "You're going to be shiny, but you've known Henna so long, I doubt she really sees you any more."

"Jared–"

"Here's what's important, Mike." He takes a long time screwing the lid back on the moisturizer. "What's important is that I know how much you worry about shit. And what's also important is that I know a big part of that worry is that, no matter what group of friends you're in, no matter how long you've known them, you always assume you're the least-wanted person there. The one everyone else could do without."

All I can do at this is swallow. I feel like I'm naked all of a sudden.

"Even when it's just you and me," he says. "I know how you worry that you need me as a friend more than I need you."

"Jared, please–"

"I've known it since we were kids, Mike. You're not the only one who worries." He play-punches me in the chest, leaving the flat of his fist there. "I wouldn't have made it without you. I got my dad and I got you and I need you both. More than you know."

I swallow again. "Thanks, man."

"I'll tell you about everything when I can," he says. "I promise. I *want* to. But talking about it, even with you, would change it and I can't risk that yet."

"Okay."

"And if you don't kiss Henna on the lips tonight *for real*, I'll make sure you have black eyes all the way through graduation."

He grins, and though I'm still worried about him – I wouldn't be me if I wasn't – the happiness I feel at what he said is just like he really did punch me in the chest.

o O o

"Would it be okay if I kissed you?" Henna asks, before we're even half a mile from her house.

I stop right there in the middle of the road.

"What?" is pretty much all I can come up with.

"It's kind of in the spirit of exploration," she says. "We've both always wondered, haven't we?"

"We have? *You* have?"

"You're a cute boy I've known for a hundred years. Of course I've thought about it."

A car pulls up behind us in the wooded dark, its headlights shining on the backs of our heads. After a second, it honks. Without taking my eyes off Henna, I hit the hazard lights. The car honks again, then pulls around us.

"Don't you feel like the world's shaken loose?" Henna says.

"Yes," I say, because it has. "You think I'm cute?"

"Here's this future we're looking at. And it's not far away like the future normally is. It's here, now. Like any second." She rubs her shoulder. "I got vaccinated for the Africa trip today. We're still going. Even when I've just had surgery on my arm. My dad says he's a doctor and can look after me and God will watch over us as we do His will and so nothing's changed. We're going and it's real."

"You could stay with us," I say and then I think, no, she probably couldn't. She knows it, too, from the look she gives me. "Or Jared. For the summer at least–"

"No," she says, shaking her head. "It's happening. There's nothing I can do about it. There's nothing I can do about graduating. Nothing I can do about going to a different college than all of my friends. Nothing I can do about these feelings for Nathan that surprise me as much as anybody. Sorry, but what's the point of lying about it? What's the point of lying about anything? We could keep being too afraid to say we don't know stuff and then the future will come and eat us anyway and we'll regret not doing all that stuff we wished we did. You know?"

"Not really."

She smiles. "There's the truth, see? Isn't it great?"

Another car passes us going the other way. It goes pretty slowly, though, and we wait for it to pass, as if it could somehow overhear our conversation.

"Why do you want to kiss me?" I ask.

"Because I don't know if I should. I don't know what it'll feel like." She shrugs. "I used to like you that way. Way back when Mel started school again. I could see how much you cared for her, Mike. How much you looked after her." Her eyes have gone a little wet. "I don't know if Teemu would have looked after me like that in the same situation." She swallows away the tears. "I'd like to think so but I'm never going to find out. And I don't like that I'm not."

I'm just staring at her. "You used to like me?"

"Yeah," she says, simply. "But I was with Tony and I also liked him. A lot. Still do. We'd have had the most incredibly pretty black Finnish Korean babies in the world."

"Why'd you break up with him then?"

She finally looks away. "He wanted us to get married this summer."

"*What?*"

"I thought about it, too. As a way to get out of the Africa trip. But then I realized that was the *only* reason I was considering it. You can't marry someone just to get away from your parents."

"People do."

"Not me, it turns out. It also made me realize I couldn't see myself marrying Tony at all. Not yet, anyway. At least not until I'd gone out and had a life of my own, where I could make my *own* decisions, maybe find out what *I* want."

"And you want to find out if you want me?"

She looks back at me. "We could have died together. But we didn't. And all I could think while we were waiting for the ambulance was how glad I was it was you with me there. Because if it was you, I didn't have to be afraid."

"I felt the same way."

"I know. I've always known." She unbuckles her seatbelt. "I *don't* know if it's the right thing for us to kiss but I don't want to leave not having found out. I'm not trying to play with your feelings and I'm so scared you might get hurt but being too afraid isn't–"

And I'm already kissing her.

She's...

Well, I don't know, you've kissed people, haven't you? So you know what the physical part is, and though we do just fine at that and the closeness and the smell of her and the taste of her mouth is so freaking amazing and though I can feel every part of where she's touching me with her non-injured hand on the back of my neck and her cast digging into my chest and, yeah, I have such a hard-on I have to readjust myself before we kiss again because it's so uncomfortable against my jeans but–

But it's really inside your head where it all happens, doesn't it?

Because I'm just thinking, *I'm kissing her I'm kissing her I'm kissing her I'm kissing Henna We're kissing It's Henna and we're kissing.*

And maybe that's stupid, but maybe it's not, maybe that's just what people do. *I'm kissing her.*

That's what I'm thinking.

There's a knock on the window so loud and surprising, we jump apart.

A car is stopped a little behind us, its headlights off. I have no reason to think so, but I have the immediate thought that it's the same car that stopped behind us before. And the same car that drove by slowly a minute ago. It turns on red and blue lights to flash at us once or twice before going dark again.

It's a police car.

"Shit," I hear Henna say.

"We haven't done anything wrong," I say.

The knock comes again and we both jump again, too. I don't think either of us are especially afraid of policemen, but two people have been killed and a zombie deer jumped over my head, so I think it's fair to say we're a little on edge.

I roll down my window. The cop is standing so close to the car, I can't even see his face at first. I do see the big truncheon-like flashlight that he knocked on the window with. It's about two inches from my head.

"Hi," I say, kind of stupidly.

"'Hi'?" he says, leaning down slow to put his head in the window. "Is that how you address an officer of the law?"

With shock, I recognize him. It's the cop who came to the school and completely failed to take us seriously when we said we'd seen indie kid Finn being chased by a little girl across the Field. He's wearing a scarf, which clearly isn't part of his uniform, and it's pitch black and he's wearing sunglasses.

We're in trouble, I think, *and not just being-stopped-by-a-cop trouble.*

"I'm waiting for an answer," he says. His words are clear and strong, nothing like the slightly drunk version we saw in the Vice Principal's office.

"I'm sorry, officer. I know we're not supposed to be–"

"No," he interrupts. "You're not."

The flashlight comes on right in my face. I flinch and I hear the cop laugh. He moves it over to Henna, who doesn't look away. She's frightened, I can tell, as frightened as me, but she's defiant, too. The accident really has shaken the world loose for her. We may be in big trouble here but if we are, she's going to look at it square on.

She's never looked more beautiful. And I'm so afraid for her I can barely keep from throwing up.

"You kids," he spits at us. "With your impudence and your sex–"

"Our what?" Henna says.

"Thinking no one understands you because you're

young. Thinking only you can see the world as it truly is." He hits the flashlight, hard, on the door of my car. "You know nothing." He hits the door again, hard enough to leave a dent. "Nothing at all." Almost casually, he smashes my wing mirror, shattering it.

"Hey!" I say, and the flashlight is suddenly bright in my face again.

"It's not safe to be out here at night," the cop says, amusement in his voice.

Still looking at the cop, I try to sneakily raise my hand to the gearshift, wondering if I can gun it and get us out of here–

"You try it," the cop says. "You just go right ahead."

"Mikey," I hear Henna whisper. She's looking out the back window.

There are policemen all around us. I don't see any cars besides the first one but there are at least twenty other cops out there, standing in a wide circle around the car, hands on holsters.

All wearing sunglasses.

I've still got my hand on the gearshift. Henna and I both glance down at it, using only our eyes.

She gives me a little nod. I'm just about to shift it–

When the voice comes. It's like a whisper mixed with the whine of a buzzsaw. It seems to come from everywhere at once, miles away but also in your head, too.

"*Look closer,*" it says, over and over, in scraping words that make both me and Henna wince. "*Look closer, look closer...*" The sound is like glass breaking against your skin, you hear it and feel it, before it vanishes, making you feel like someone's touched you in a wrong way.

The cop turns off his flashlight. I hear Henna breathing, and I reach out in the darkness to take her hand. She must hear me breathing, too, because she's already reaching out to take mine.

The cop takes off his sunglasses.

In the pitch darkness, his eyes are glowing. Glowing blue. Just like the deer.

All around us in the night, the other cops take off their sunglasses, too. A circle of glowing blue eyes watch us in the silence.

"Go," Henna whispers. "Just go."

I shift into drive, but the cop's hand shoots in *way*

faster than should be possible and grips my arm, hard enough to hurt.

And he's pointing his gun in my face.

For a long minute, all I can see is the barrel of that gun.

"You aren't the ones we want," he frowns, sounding disappointed. He lowers the gun, puts his sunglasses back on and moves away. Out there, in the darkness, the blue lights disappear two by two.

I don't wait. I step on the gas and with a burning of wheels, we race off into the night.

"Mike," Henna says.

"I know," I say.

"Mike," she says again, just saying my name, not asking anything. I don't even know where I'm going, I'm just driving as fast as I can away and away.

I hear Henna say, "I've never been so happy not to be an indie kid in my entire life."

She starts crying, and we do that for a while, just drive and cry.

Mainly out of relief for being alive.

CHAPTER THE TENTH, *in which indie kids Joffrey and Earth disappear from their homes, their bodies found miles away; Satchel goes into hiding at an abandoned drive-in with fellow indie kids Finn, Dylan, Finn, Finn, Lincoln, Archie, Wisconsin, Finn, Aquamarine, and Finn; seeing a blue light in the night, Satchel meets the boy from the amulet, the handsomest one she's ever seen; he tells her this isn't a safe place for her or the others and that they should run; then he tells her she's beautiful in her own special way and that's when she knows she can trust him; the indie kids go back to their homes.*

◄O►

Things get darker in the days after the cop incident.

There are two more dead indie kids. I didn't

really know either of them, except to see them in the hallway at school, but still. "This is worse than when they were all dying beautifully of cancer," Henna said, and she's right.

The cops are calling one a suicide and the other a car accident.

The cops are saying this.

And why should we doubt the cops?

Henna and I told Mel and Jared and, fine, Nathan what happened, but none of us told our parents. How could we? My dad's automatically out of everything important. (I'm not even sure I've seen him this week, just evidence – discarded clothes, snoring – that he's in the house somewhere.) My mom's in pre-campaign mode, which is probably not the best time to tell her the local policemen have gone crazy and are threatening her son. (I told her I broke the mirror hitting a mailbox; she just sighed and handed me the insurance forms.) Henna's parents would pack her off to a convent, and even Mr Shurin would be overly concerned and get involved in all the wrong ways.

We're just going to stick together and tough it out

and try to live long enough to graduate. The usual.

The surviving indie kids disappeared from school for a bit. No one knows where they went. No one knows what they saw there. No one knows why they all came back on the Friday.

They won't tell us what's going on, even when we ask them.

"What'd they say?" Jared asks Mel over lunch.

"That we wouldn't understand," Mel says, frowning like she's about to fire the world from a job it loves. "But one of them showed me a poem about how we're all essentially alone. As if they're not the biggest clique of togetherness that ever was."

Everyone knows the indie kids don't use the internet – have you noticed? They never do, it's weird, like it never occurs to them, like it's still 1985 and there's only card catalogues – so we can't find them discussing anything online. The vibe seems to be that it's totally not our business. Historically, non-indie kids were pretty much left alone by the vampires and the soul-eating ghosts, so maybe they have a point.

But the deer who caused our accident. And the zombie deer coming out of Henna's car. And the scary cops. It's like when adults say world news isn't our worry. Why the hell isn't it?

"They don't look like you," Mel says, when the prints of my senior photos come in. "I mean, not even a little."

I didn't bother with digital files; I knew they were going to be gruesome. The prints are meant to go into my graduation announcements, the ones with that pointless extra bit of tissue paper and double envelope you send to relatives in the hope they send back money. But maybe even that's out.

"You could be your second cousin, maybe," Henna says, leaning against the counter at the drugstore. We've stopped by Mel's work to check up on her, even though it's broad daylight on a Saturday afternoon.

"We don't have *any* cousins," I say. "Dad's an only child and Uncle Rick doesn't have kids."

Henna blinks. "I've got like forty."

"Excuse me," a skinny, scraggly man says behind us.

"For methadone you need to talk to the pharmacist," Mel says, without even looking up from the photos.

"You're not the pharmacist?" the man asks.

We all turn to him. He kind of freaks out at the attention, pulling his arms around the heavy-metal T-shirt that hangs from his collarbones and shuffling away to the pharmacy counter at the back.

"Poor guy," Mel says. She goes back to my pictures. "You look like a court artist's drawing of yourself on the stand."

Henna gasps. "You *do* look like that."

I move closer to her, pretending to get nearer to my photos. I brush my arm against her arm. It's elementary school shit, but she doesn't move away. It's been over a week since the cops stopped us, but we haven't kissed again or even really talked about it. We've spent a lot of time together, but all in the company of our friends. Still, the thing with the cops was so threatening and bizarre and unexplained, it made kissing seem kind of childish. For the moment, at least.

"At least you can't see the scar," I say.

Jared's hands have helped the stitches already come out, but without slabs of make-up, there's still a hoof-made gash in my face. It'll heal more, I know, but the scar ain't going anywhere.

"It's going to be fine," Mel says. "Once the redness is gone, it might even look kind of amazing."

"Nobody really sees scars after the first time," Henna says. "Not anyone who matters, anyway."

"Yeah," I say, flatly, "people who make fun of my face probably aren't my friends."

Henna reaches up and traces her fingers lightly over it, running down from the tip below my cheekbone, over the wider part on the flat of my cheek, to the little curlicue on the side of my chin. "It's still you," she says. "Everyone will be able to see *you*."

She keeps her fingers there for a second. Yeah, I really want to kiss her again.

"Um," the scraggly man says, back at the main counter while his prescription gets filled. "Could I get a pack of Marlboro?"

Mel grabs a pack off the rows of cancer-addled faces and tumoured lungs in the racks behind her and rings it up. The man is still so obviously shy of us, he fumbles with his money, dropping a five-dollar bill on the ground. I lean to get it, but Henna's better placed. She lifts it up to him.

"I know you," the man whispers, not looking her in the face. He slides the five plus another ten at my sister.

"You do?" Henna asks.

The man looks at her once, then away again, shyly. "Teemu," he says.

Henna slumps like her clothes suddenly weigh an extra hundred pounds. "Erik?" she says. "Erik Peddersen?"

The scraggly man nods.

"Oh, Jesus," Henna says, under her breath, but out of surprise, not scorn. The scraggly man blushes anyway.

"Strange shit going on," he says, still not making eye contact.

"I don't think it's vampires," Henna says.

"No," Erik says, firmly. "They'd have come for me if it was."

There's an empty, silent moment, where no one's blinking and Erik is obviously growing more uncomfortable. Then "Number Nine," says the voice of Pratip, the pharmacist, over the loudspeaker, and Erik immediately heads off without looking at us again. We watch him go.

"Friend of your brother's?" Mel gently asks.

"In his band," Henna says. "Haven't seen him since it all ended. Guess he had a hard time coping."

She pulls her good arm into herself, almost visibly shrinking. I put my own arm around her, and she leans into me. I kind of hate myself for thinking how nice it is.

"That won't be us," Mel says, meaning Erik. "Whatever happens, that's not going to be us."

And she says it like she's demanding a promise.

"Your sister is like a cute little robot," Tina, our manager, says. "I just want to eat her right up."

Meredith sits alone at a booth in Grillers. Jared's piled the table in front of her – the part not covered in homework and school hardware – with enough cheesy toast and blueberry lemonade to ruin every Jazz & Tap class she's ever taken.

"I want a kid," Tina says, looking at her hungrily from the waitress station.

"Get one from Ronald," Jared says, stealing a fry from a plate.

"He's *infertile*." She whispers it louder than her normal speaking voice.

"You should adopt," Jared says. "Adoption is a moral good."

Tina makes a face. "Yeah, because Ronald's exactly the kind of guy who makes a good impression on a social worker." She sighs, looking around Grillers. "Grumpy night. Everyone's in a bad mood."

She's right about that. I've had more complaints tonight than I've had in the last six months. One guy even sent back his *water*.

"There's a weird feeling in the air, isn't there?" Tina says. "All those kids killing themselves at the high school." Jared and I exchange a look but don't correct her. "You can feel it when you're driving home at night. God knows what could be out there in those woods."

Tina would have been twenty or so when the soul-eating ghosts came, so just that little bit too old to be directly involved. Still, you always wonder how much people know and just don't say. Or pretend not to know. Or purposely forget.

Meredith leans out of her booth to catch my eye, even though she sat in Jared's section. He's more generous with the blueberry lemonade. I go over to her.

"What's up?"

She shows me her pad and swipes through a bunch of web pages. "There's nothing about it on the main news sites, not even if you search."

"You shouldn't be looking anyway. Leave it to me and Mel to take care of–"

"But if you go to the right places," she says, ignoring me and opening a few locked-door discussion rooms on weird boards for things like obscure Japanese toys and underground video games. She turns the pad to me, several windows open.

I want to keep scolding her, but I can't help but scan the pages. Lots of references to *blue eyes* and *indie kids dying* and *the Immortals*. Lots about *the Immortals*.

"Most of it's speculation," Meredith says.

"'Immortals' could mean a lot of things, but people are thinking maybe a kind of multi-dimensional thing. Or elves. Or angels, even. And the blue lights are an energy that kills you or brings you back to life or something. I'll bet that's what the deer were running from." She sinks her chin down to her hands on the table. "Nobody knows for sure because the indie kids aren't talking to anybody but themselves. It's happening a lot of places, though. In some version or another."

"Just like the vampires," I say, almost to myself. Then I see her worried little face. "But you've got nothing to worry about. They never come after little mites like you."

"What if they cancel Bolts of Fire?" she asks, and you might think this is a ten year old asking a selfish question when people are dying. Not Meredith. She's asking if everything's going to be all right. It probably will be, but when did "probably" ever help anyone?

"Jeesh, people are cranky tonight," Jared says, coming over with the coffee pots. "Want anything else, Merde Breath?"

"Fresh cheesy toast?" she asks in a small voice.

Jared smiles. "Coming right up. Mel and Henna just pulled in by the way." He glances at me. "Nathan's with them."

I take the coffee pots from him and walk back to my side of the restaurant. Tina's already pouring out a Ronald tale of woe to Mel and Henna by the front door. "...and his toenails are like something out of a fable–"

"Hey," I say. They say "Hey" back. It's kind of like verbal tag, isn't it? Hey, here I am, are you here with me, Yes, we are here with you, and everyone feels good because "Hey".

I tip my head to Meredith's booth. "She's worrying. Looking stuff up."

Mel sighs. "I told her not to, but I'm not surprised." She heads over to our little sister.

"Staff discount on whatever you guys want," Tina says. "Make *somebody* happy."

"Thanks, Tina," I say. She smiles and just stands there, looking at me and Henna. Then looking some more. Then looking some more. Then finally saying, "Oh!" and heading off to force more cheesy toast on customers.

"You okay?" I ask Henna when Tina's gone.

"Yeah, you?"

"Good. Weird. Good."

She smiles. "Me, too."

I swallow. "Listen, Henna–"

"I know. Unfinished business." She looks down at her cast, covered in ink by all the signatures. The biggest one is Jared's. The smallest one is mine, but it's the only one she allowed on the palm of her hand. "I've been thinking," she says. "Do you remember what I said, just before we hit the deer?"

Oh, shit. "Not really."

She knows I'm lying, but doesn't say. "You said you loved me. And I said I didn't think that was true."

"You don't know that."

"But I don't think you know it either, Mikey." She taps her cast. "I do want to kiss you again, though."

I half-grin. "In the name of exploration?"

"Three of your tables want their bills," Tina says, reappearing. "They seem kinda pissy about it, too."

Henna's already heading over to Mel and Meredith, who are lengthily pretending to order from Jared. "I thought Nathan was with you," I say, as she goes.

"Still outside," she says, shrugging.

And I wonder if she's kissed *him* in the name of exploration.

I get my three tables their bills. Only one of them leaves me a tip. I seat an angry-looking older couple who are already asking about the senior discount before they're even in their chairs, and this regular fireman who comes in every Saturday, orders the same thing, and just asks to be left alone as long as the all-you-can-eat shrimp keeps coming. I look back at Meredith's booth as I punch in their orders.

Still no Nathan.

I check around for Tina, then step outside, wiping my hands on a towel, feeling the pull of a loop that I want to wash and wash and wash them. I don't see Nathan anywhere, just oil stains, the traffic-resistant pine shrubs that border us, and a big open sky with a full moon beaming down. I head around towards the garbage area, two big bins in a little brick hut that Jared and I are inevitably scheduled to wheel out every Sunday night. They smell unbelievably bad, even after we pour buckets of bleach into them.

There's no one there either. I keep walking, still

wiping my hands – just being near the garbage area would do that to even a normal person – not sure why I'm so curious or what I'm even thinking. I don't even like Nathan.

I probably wouldn't want to see him killed, though.

I'm beginning to get properly worried – I'm going to wipe my fingerprints off with this rag – when I turn the last corner and see him, his back against the brick of the restaurant outside the emergency exit. He's having a cigarette, but he doesn't look like he's hurrying.

I stop in a shadow. Still wiping my hands, yes, but trying not to make a thing of it.

Nathan's got a funny old face when no one's looking at it. Like he's almost an entirely different person, the saddest person I've ever seen – which is saying something – and sure, he lost his sister and he moves around a lot and he used to be an indie kid–

He used to be an indie kid. The little "mascot", he said.

And it's because I don't like him, albeit just for stupid, jealous reasons, but the first thing I think isn't:

Maybe we could get him to find out what's going on from some of our indie kids here.

It's: *What does he know that he's not telling us?*

Because he made a joke out of it, didn't he? He showed up and the indie kids started dying. Someone clever would point that out themselves and say how worried they were that they'd start being blamed, especially if they *were* to blame.

But then, so would someone who really did show up innocently.

He grinds his cigarette out with his foot. Then he picks up the butt and looks around for somewhere to throw it away so he's not littering, which, okay, is maybe not the action of a killer.

Still.

He throws it in a trashcan down by a car, then stands looking into the windows of the restaurant. He doesn't do anything, doesn't wave at anyone or try to catch anyone's attention, despite having a view of almost all of Jared's section and definitely the booth where Meredith, Mel and Henna sit.

He looks sad again. Or sad still, whatever. He turns into the night, gazing at the cars driving by, at the stars and moon that still shine there.

What are you waiting for, former indie kid?

With a sigh, he disappears behind the other side of the restaurant, heading towards the entrance. Where, once inside, he'll no doubt pass the pissed-off seniors and annoyed fireman who are wondering where the hell their waiter's got to.

I hurry back in, still wiping my hands, wondering what I've seen. Wondering if I've seen *anything*. I probably haven't.

But what was he doing out there? And what do we know about him, really?

CHAPTER THE ELEVENTH, *in which Satchel, mourning her friends but pressing on feistily, keeps researching her amulet with the card catalogue; the mysterious boy appears in her bedroom one night and his first words are, "I'm sorry"; he tells her he is the Prince in the Court of the Immortals; his mother, the Empress, wants to take over this world, sensing great food here to feed their immortality; they seek to open more fissures, find more permanent Vessels in which to live, but the Prince has fallen in love with Satchel from afar and can't stand idly by while her world is enslaved; "I've come to help," he says; they kiss.*

◄O►

"And so it is with great pleasure and excitement," my mom says, standing at the podium, smiling into the bright lights of the cameras, "that I announce my candidacy to represent the people of the Eighth Congressional District of the great state of Washington."

There's applause from her supporters and from the party officials gathered around her. She smiles back at us, but just with her mouth, and I realize my dad is the only one of us clapping along. I elbow Mel, and she and I and Meredith start slapping our hands together, looking like the perfect family we totally aren't. I'm even wearing a suit.

Mom's satisfied and turns back to the cameras. In truth, there aren't all that many. There's one main feed that'll supply footage to the network affiliates if they want it, one camera from the local independent station that mostly shows reruns, and another supplied by the party itself for internet campaigning. There are some print and web journalists, too, but all in all, I think interested public are outnumbered by politicians and family.

"State Senator Mitchell?" a local journalist asks when the applause has died down.

"You don't really need the 'State' in front

of it, Ed," my mom says, smiling wide.

"What do you have to say about Tom Shurin, your expected opponent?" Ed the journalist continues.

"I say that I welcome a vigorous and clean campaign based on the issues I outlined in my speech," my mom says, smiling like a president. You may not like politicians much – I don't – but she's good at her job. I can't remember a single one of the issues from her speech, only the vague sense that she really cared about them. Which she once told me is the perfect result. If you're too specific, people will purposely mishear you so they can be outraged about whatever thing that usually outrages them. You want to get them on your side emotionally, apparently, where they ask fewer questions.

They want us a bit dumb and a bit afraid. Which for the most part, I think we are.

"What about the rest of your family, Alice?" a nastier voice says. I recognize it. It's this woman who runs a bitter-but-annoyingly-significant little blog about how local politicians are morons for not agreeing with everything she thinks. "We wouldn't want a repeat of the tragedies that scuttled your run for Lieutenant Governor."

I see Mel's face set in some fairly unfiltered hatred that I hope the cameras aren't capturing, but my mom doesn't miss a beat. "I have a normal American family, Cynthia, and just like any family, we try to face our challenges with grace and dignity. I love my children more than anything in the world, and I would *never* do this if I didn't have their complete support."

I wonder if that's true.

"And," my mother goes on, her voice actually emotional, "I would take great issue if any press decided to go after my children." Her voice goes tough, but it's politician tough, and I wonder again if it's true. "They'd have one ferocious mama bear to deal with first."

Her campaign team bursts into spontaneous applause.

"How you holding up, Dad?" Mel asks him as the press conference winds down.

"Hmm?" he says, looking at her vaguely. He's in

a suit as well, of course, and from the smell of him, reasonably sober. He takes a drink of the coffee provided while my mom does a few friendly interviews. "Oh, you know," he says. "Another year, another campaign." He pats his pockets, but doesn't look like he expects to find anything there. "We'll get by."

My mom comes over in her power blue dress and her power pearl necklace. "Thank you," she says, and it's so genuine, we all feel a little embarrassed. "You did great."

"You're welcome," Mel says, wary as ever. "Mama bear, huh?"

My mom gives a tight smile. "I'm really not going to let them get to you, Melinda. You have my word."

"You can't control that," Mel says, "but thanks. It's a small race, I don't think they'll bother." My mother stiffens a little at "small race" and Mel immediately closes her eyes. "Not what I meant."

"I know," my mom says. "You two will be out of here before it really heats up."

It's the first time she's acknowledged this. She sounds kind of sad.

"We'll get by," I hear myself saying. "We'll get by."

oOo

We've taken separate cars to get here; my mom coming up from the capital with her team, my dad under orders to clean up enough to get there for the evening. He can do it, if you push him, and my mom really, really knows how to push him. Who knows what their secret married life is like? I can't even imagine it, don't ever want to, and feel like I have less clue about it as time passes. But whatever, it seems to work for them.

Mel drives Dad and Meredith back home. I ride with my mom.

"The best thing is that it's only six months to the election so it's a short campaign," my mom says, pushing on through the dark. "Normally for a seat this big, I'd have had to be running for at least the last year." She glances over at me. "Which would have been worse."

"You'd still have run, though."

"Yeah. Yeah, I probably would have. And you and your sister judge me for that, I know."

"We don't judge you."

To my surprise, she snorts. "Yes, you do. I judged *my* parents. That's what young people do, isn't it?"

Her parents live in North Dakota. I've met them about four times in seventeen years of life. I wonder if she just kept on judging them.

"I do all this for you guys, you know," she says. "I know you think it's just ambition and power-seeking, and well, for goodness' sake, I'm a politician and I wouldn't be a politician if those things weren't there, too, but it's not just that."

I don't know what to say. She *never* talks like this. Never hints that there's anything behind her motivations other than pure, patriotic public service. "Are you feeling okay?" I ask.

"The thing is, I'm not even surprised you'd ask that. We've forgotten how to talk to each other, haven't we? Funny how things evolve and evolve and then one day, you look up and they're different."

"You don't believe in evolution."

She laughs. Actually *laughs*. "Well, not politically, I don't." She looks over at me again. "I wonder what you think of me. *Really*. What kind of a person am I when seen by you?"

I keep quiet, hoping like hell this is a rhetorical question. It is.

"I *am* feeling okay," she says. "But I'm also stepping into the big time, son. This isn't local government with all its little tyrants and petty feuds. This is national office."

"Which has big tyrants and dangerous feuds."

"Absolutely," she sighs. "I thought it was all over with the Lieutenant Governor's race, that I'd be in local office forever. Maybe end up on a school board some day or a state commission for something or other. But all of a sudden, in the space of a few weeks, here it all is. The big show."

"If you win."

"I will."

Yeah, she probably will.

"What do you *do* when your dreams are about to come true?" she asks. "No one ever tells you. They tell you to chase them, but what happens when you actually catch one?"

"You enjoy it. Do your best, try not to be a dick."

"Language." But she's not upset. "I really do this for you guys, though, whatever you may believe. They're *my* dreams, yes, but they're dreams of a world I can make better for you."

"Us specifically? Me and Mel and Meredith?"

"Your generation. I know you guys face some tough things."

"Do you?"

"I want to help with that."

"Do you?"

"Quit saying that. I was a teenager once, too. I know what goes on."

"You do?" I risk.

She frowns at me. She looks in the rear-view mirror, checking out for Mel in the car behind us. "I saw stuff you wouldn't believe," she says, under her breath.

My ears prick. "What stuff?" I ask, carefully.

She just shakes her head. "The world isn't safe, Mike. It just isn't. I wish it was, but it's not. I worry for you and Mel. I worry myself sick for Meredith, that the future's going to have enough for her to be happy and protected."

"You need to let her go to the Bolts of Fire concert."

"I know. She deserves it. She's going to miss you two so much."

I leave that alone, because it doesn't feel like it belongs to her. Trees pass us by in the night. I watch them, looking for strange blue lights, I guess, but not finding any.

"What stuff did you see?" I ask again. "When you were a teenager?"

"Nothing," she says, too quickly. "Are you ready for your finals?"

"Yes. What do you mean, nothing?"

"Mike," she says, warning. "The mistake of every young person is to think they're the only ones who see darkness and hardship in the world."

"That's what the cop said," I mumble.

"What cop?" she snaps.

"On TV," I say, pleased at myself for thinking so fast. "The mistake of every adult, though, is to think darkness and hardship aren't important to young people because we'll grow out of it. Who cares if we will? Life is happening to us *now*, just like it's happening to you."

"What's happening to you now?" she says, her voice changing, alert as a meerkat.

"Mom–"

"Tell me. Are you okay?"

"I didn't mean–"

"I think you did mean," she says. "Teens argue with their parents. That's the law of nature. Doesn't mean we stop caring about you. Doesn't mean we stop being parents."

"Dad stopped. A long time ago."

There's a really, *really* dangerous silence at this. I find that I don't actually care.

"Your father..." she starts, but she doesn't finish.

"He checked out after he stole all that money from Uncle Rick," I say. "He never checked back in. Mel loves him, still. So where did he go?"

"And why can't I bring him back? I don't know. I wish I did. He was there *tonight*."

"He was about forty per cent there tonight, and the sad thing is, we all thought that was a victory."

She doesn't say anything to this, just stares ahead into the darkened road. I feel bad now for wrecking the mood on her big announcement night, though I'm still wondering what she saw as a teenager. Was that the time of the undead? No, that was a bit later.

But was there *something*, in her teenage years? Why have I never thought that she might have seen all this stuff, too?

"You didn't say what was happening with you," she says. "I need to know. I *want* to know. Not for the campaign. Because I'm your mother."

I don't answer her. I don't want to.

But then I do.

"I think I need to see a psychiatrist again," I say. "I think I need to go back on medication."

There's the smallest of pauses, like she's slotting the information into some grid in her head. "The compulsive stuff?" she asks.

"Yep."

"It's gotten that bad?"

"It's gotten really, really bad."

I watch her absorb this. I watch her nod. "Okay."

"'Okay'?" I say, surprised.

"Of course," she says, also surprised. "Why wouldn't it be?"

"Well … the campaign, for one–"

"Didn't you hear me? Weren't you listening to that ferocious mama bear crap?"

"I assumed that was something the party wrote for you in case you got asked about Mel."

"Well. Okay. That's true. But–"

"Lieutenant Governor would have been the big time, too. And that's when everything went to hell. You can't blame us for being a little weirded out by it."

"No," she says, after a second. "No, I can't. Is it *because* of the campaign? Your ... trouble?"

"I don't think so. It started before Mankiewicz died. This isn't me trying to tell you not to run. I think it's just ... life and graduation and everything changing."

And zombie deer, I don't say. And kids at my school dying. And Henna and her spirit of exploration.

"We'll work it out," she says. "I promise. I'll talk to my team and work something out."

"Why does your team need to know?"

"They need to know everything a journalist might find out. That way they can protect us."

We're nearly home, and I don't say anything more. I certainly don't ask what it might be like for families that don't need protection from their parent's jobs.

Strange. It feels like we'd almost got somewhere, but then missed it. I'm surprised at how disappointed I feel.

When I go to bed, there's a text from Jared. *Not bad in a suit there, Mikey.*

I text back. *You saw it? Was it gruesome?*

Jared: *All politics is/are gruesome.*

Me: *Will you have to be at your dad's?*

Jared: *He doesn't get a press conference. He's announcing on Twitter.*

Me: *Oh. Sorry.*

Jared: *Don't be. Makes him seem like the undergod.*

Me: *Did you just type undergod?*

Jared: *Underdog.*

Me: *Does anyone use Twitter any more?*

Jared: *UNDERDOG.*

Before I put my phone away, I text Mel. *You all right?*

Counting the days, she texts back from her bedroom.

Me: *Dad was okay.*

She doesn't answer.

Me: *I like Call Me Steve.*

Mel: *Me too.*

I put my phone back on my side table to go to sleep, but it buzzes again.

Mel: *What's going to happen to Meredith when we go?*

Me: *She'll be better than all of us. The only one who won't need therapy.*

Mel: *I don't trust ANYONE who doesn't need therapy.*

Me: *You don't trust anyone period.*

Mel: *I trust you.*

CHAPTER THE TWELFTH, *in which Satchel's love for the Prince grows real and true and like nothing she's ever known before; second indie kid Finn feels her distance and is hurt, but she tells him, "No one can provide the heart its own peace; you have to find it yourself"; Dylan, to her surprise, is the one who gives her space; even better, no one else has died; they follow the Prince's instructions on where and when to be, and all danger is avoided; Satchel and the Prince kiss again, but he respects her too much to demand more.*

◄o►

The word "finals" makes it sound like a bigger deal than it is, at least for us. We're all College Prep, so most of the hard work had to be done early enough to prove to colleges we'd be worth indebting ourselves forever to them. The "final" for US History was just that Civil War essay, for example, which we all managed to get turned in on time, splitting the questions so me and Mel didn't do the same one. The rest of our major tests have at least two of us in each class, so lunches turn into study sessions. For me, my only real worries are Calc and English.

"What is the limit as x approaches one of one minus x-squared over x to the fourth minus x?" I read.

"Iambic pentameter," Mel says.

"You are?"

"Minus two-thirds," Henna answers.

We look up to Jared. "Yep," he says.

"It's not iambic pentameter?" Mel says.

"You're *definitely* bic pentameter," Henna says. "In those shoes, anyway."

"Because they look like four feet?" Mel says.

"Can I squeeze in?" Nathan says, appearing at our table.

Why does he do that? Always arrive late? He never comes *with* anyone, just wanders in after we're all together. What's he up to?

"I brought that essay I did last year on *Zen and the Art of Motorcycle Maintenance*," he says, handing it to me. Me and Mel are the only two in AP English, and that awful, awful book is one of our exam texts, so he's really helping us out here.

"Thanks," I say, a bit surly.

"Don't be too thankful, I only got a B and I still don't have a clue what the hell the book was about."

"No one does," Mel says. "I think that's the point."

"Did you even finish it?" I ask her.

She hesitates. "Ish."

"Listen–" Nathan says.

"This is…" I say, flipping through his essay. "Long."

"They called it Core College in Tulsa," he says, "and they really weren't kidding. Listen–"

"Let me see," Mel says, reaching over for the essay.

"Is this right?" Henna asks Jared, showing him some Calc work. He scans it in an instant.

"All fine," he says. "I don't know why you're worried, Henna. You're as good as me."

"Meredith isn't even as good as you," she says, frowning at her paper.

"Guys?" Nathan says.

"Crap," Mel says, reading his essay. "This is really smart. Like *really* smart. So much smarter than me."

"I doubt that," I say.

"What is this word even?" She points on the page, holding it up.

"Ossification," Nathan says.

"What kind of sixteen-year-old writes 'ossification'?" Mel says, her voice ticking up in slight panic. "Why do *I* not use 'ossification'?!"

"I was seventeen, actually. I'm eighteen now."

"Me, too," says Henna.

"Me, too," says Jared.

"I'm *nineteen*," says Mel, "and I know nothing of ossification."

I'll be eighteen in June. Jared is only two months older than me, but I'd sort of forgotten that this was the two months where I'm at least a whole year younger than everyone else. Including, it seems, Nathan, who's still trying to ask us something.

"I'd like to paint the bridge," he says and

everyone looks at him, shocked. "If you guys would do it with me."

It's a senior tradition to paint the railroad bridge near the school. Buses, students and staff all drive under it every morning to reach the school gates. Most of the things written there are boring ("Gina, Joelle, Stefanie, Friends 4Evah" (yes, seriously, 4Evah)), stupid ("Here I paint all broken-hearted" and then they didn't leave enough room to finish the poem) or vulgar/threatening ("Andersen sucks dicks"; Andersen being our wildly unliked shop teacher and basketball coach who probably never, in fact, engages in the behaviour in question). The tags get painted over by other boring, stupid, or obscene tags in a matter of days, but it's tradition, as if that alone is reason enough. Slavery and buying your wife were traditions, too.

It's also technically illegal, of course, so it has to be done at night, usually deep in the darkest part. We were never going to do it anyway – we're exactly the sort of nice kids who would consider it too stupid to bother; Jared didn't even do it with the football team when we beat our district rival in the last game (to finish the season 2-7, woohoo, go team) – but with all the blue-eyed cops, the blue-eyed deer, and indie kids dying from probably blue-eyed causes, it was definitely out of the question.

Until Nathan suggested it.

"You're not even from here," I said, over that study lunch, but I was already too late. I could see the eyes of the others light up.

"Exactly," Nathan said. "I'm not from *anywhere*. I've got nothing. No traditions. No friends except you guys, and you," he said to me, "don't even like me."

I waited too long to protest.

"I just," he said, shrugging, "I want something I did in high school to be … high school-y. So I can look back in fifty years and say, 'At least I did something stupid and young as proof that I was there.'"

And that kinda cracked it. Henna agreed immediately, Mel said his story made her sad but not doing it would now make her sadder, and Jared said, "Why not?"

"Because zombie deer," I say now, shivering even

though it's not actually all that cold, even in the middle of the night. We're in my car again, parked a block away from the rail bridge. "And cops with murder in their eyes. And actual dead people."

"There's enough of us," Jared says, squashed in the back seat with Nathan and Mel. Henna gets the passenger seat because of her still-broken arm and because she's Henna. "We'll be careful and we'll be all right."

Nathan holds up his backpack. "I got five cans. One colour for each of us. Nearly got arrested."

"Nearly doesn't count," I say.

"Silver, gold, blue, red and yellow." He looks at me in the rear-view mirror. "You get yellow."

"Are we going to do this or not?" Mel yawns.

"I vote not," I say.

"*Enough*, Mikey," Henna says, scornfully enough to make my stomach hurt. She gets out of the car. The back seat follows her and I'm last, looking like I'm pouting as I accept the can of yellow paint.

The bridge isn't actually all that big, crossing just two lanes of an old logging road. There are embankments either side leading up to it, and people sometimes paint the concrete ledges of these, too. We don't. We don't want to waste any time. I follow Henna up the right embankment where she's walking with Mel. Jared and Nathan head up the other side. The idea is you stand on the bridge and lean over the top, writing whatever you want from above.

There's a lot of shaking of paint cans, a lot of the metallic pinging sound of the ball-bearing they leave inside to stir the paint.

"We don't have white," I whisper, loud enough for everyone to hear. "You're supposed to have white to paint over what went before."

"Not if you're creative enough," Nathan says. He's already reached the far end of the bridge, and with his can of gold paint, he turns a shoddily painted cardinal – our sad school mascot; I've never seen a live one the whole of my life I've lived in this state – into, I'll admit it, a fairly nifty-looking bumblebee. I see Jared nod in appreciation, and my irritated stomach growls some more.

Mel's got the dark blue and has made her way to the middle of the bridge, leaning over decisively and painting "A Year Too Late" in puffy blue letters over some streaked puffy pink ones that obviously got rained on.

"Do you really believe that?" I ask her.

"Oh," she says, "I had no idea this was about what we really *believed*." She pops the cap back on her paint can, takes out her phone, and starts texting Call Me Steve, who's on nights.

I lean out over the bridge to see what Nathan's finishing up. The bumblebee now flies away from a golden arm that it's just stung. "Leave Your Sting Behind", he writes.

"Bees die when they do that," I say. Henna nudges me, annoyed.

"It's a metaphor," Nathan says.

"Metaphorical bees die, too."

Jared's at work with the silver paint, covering up a heart celebrating the no doubt eternal love of Oliver and Shania. He takes the gold paint from Nathan and sprays a circle and some markings against the still-wet bed of silver.

"What's that?" Nathan asks.

"Kind of my own personal tag," Jared says.

I don't recognize it, but I can see a line of cats stopped just outside the streetlight down the road. I wonder if it's a kind of standing blessing for them, as long as it lasts. They don't come any closer, and I also wonder if they know Jared doesn't want them to. No one's told Nathan that anything's different about Jared. It's a pact we all silently keep. Who'd believe us anyway? Indie kids are dying before their eyes and no one's even guessing at what's probably the real reason. These Immortals that Meredith found. Or not. But it sure as hell isn't accident or suicide.

"Why are you in such a bad mood?" Henna says to me, shaking her can of red paint.

I shrug, still pouty.

"I like Nathan," she says.

"I know. I've heard all about your uncontrollable attraction."

"And I like *you*, Mike, though not very much tonight, I have to say."

"There's something up with him. Where did he come from? Why does he always join us late? Why doesn't he–?"

"Jealousy makes you ugly."

"And assuming this is all about *you* makes *you* ugly," I hiss.

She turns from me, furious, and leans over the bridge, can at the ready.

But she doesn't spray anything.

"Look," she says, stepping back.

It's hard to see in the way the streetlight is angled at us, but there are markings along the top of the railing of the bridge. Words.

"Names," Mel says, looking close.

"Finn," Henna reads, "Kerouac, Joffrey, Earth." She looks at Mel. "It's the indie kids who died."

"But why up here?" Jared says. "Where no one can see them?"

I look at Nathan. "Maybe it's the killers," I say, still annoyed. "Maybe they put the names up here as trophies. Maybe this is the most dangerous place we could have come tonight."

"Would you *stop* it?" Henna says. She touches the names on the railing. The paint is black, simple. Just names.

"Look," Nathan says, kneeling down. At our feet are small flowers, little more than tiny wild flowers,

189

really, but different kinds, spread along the side of the rail tracks under the names of the dead indie kids.

Henna touches them, softly. "I'll bet this is their way of remembering them. A kind of memorial." She stands. "One that no one can see, but that they know is here."

"No one's painted over it," Jared says.

"Or kicked away the flowers," Mel says. "I wonder if everyone knows about this except us?"

"I don't feel like painting anything any more," Henna says, handing her can back to Nathan. "Feels like tagging inside a church."

I'm still holding my can of yellow paint. "I didn't want to come and now you're telling me I can't even make my own tag?"

Henna frowns. They all frown. I frown, too, what the hell. I'm having one of those days where I can't seem to say anything right, so screw it.

"Fine," I say, throwing the can at Nathan harder than really necessary. "Let's just go home."

"Oh, shit," Henna says, looking past me. I turn, and we all look.

Down the train tracks, deep in the dark wooded

area where they disappear, a whole crowd of glowing blue eyes is approaching.

Henna is already running, scrambling down the embankment, trying to keep her balance with one arm. I run after her, checking only to see that Mel and Jared are running, too. Nathan's lagging behind, staring into the darkness at the eyes.

"What are they?" he says.

"Just run, you moron!" I shout, grabbing Henna as she stumbles and practically dragging her towards my car. I shove her in the passenger seat and open the back doors for Mel and Jared as I run around the car as fast as I can. I hop behind the wheel and start the engine. Jared and Mel get inside.

Nathan is only just coming down the embankment.

"Don't leave him!" Henna says, alarmed, as I put the car in gear.

And for a moment there, just for a second, I almost do leave him. He's running. He looks as frightened as any of us.

But.

"Whose idea was this?" I spit. "We would *never* have been here if it hadn't been for him!"

"Mikey–" Jared starts.

"I'm going." I take my foot off the brake, but Nathan runs right in front of the car. He jumps in beside Jared, who's kept his door open.

"Go! Go! Go!" Nathan yells, and I step on the gas.

I shoot under the bridge, past the high school. There's nothing much back here, but there's a longer way home we can take. I speed there now, careening around a corner too fast. Everyone screams as we skid, but I correct it and we're already sailing past the gym.

"I don't think they're coming after us," Nathan says, looking out the back window.

"And how do you know that, *Nathan*?" I say.

He looks at me, confused. "What?"

"Why did you drag us all out to the bridge tonight? Were you going to feed us to them? Is that what happened to the indie kids?"

"Mike–" Henna says.

"Who are you?" I shout into the rear-view mirror,

going way too fast down a darkened road. "Where the hell did you come from?"

"I told you," Nathan said, still looking confused. "Tulsa and Portland and–"

I slam on the brakes, making everybody scream again. "Get the hell out of my car!"

"Mike!" Henna says, more strongly.

"WHAT?" I roar at her.

"It was my idea," she says.

The car is quiet. The motor vibrating. That's the only sound.

"What?" I say again.

"The bridge was my idea," she says. "Nathan was feeling down and I told him about the tradition and that we should see if anyone wanted to do it."

"She said you'd probably say no," Nathan says, looking wounded. "So I offered to ask, because it'd be less embarrassing if you turned *me* down."

"That's what happened, Mikey," Henna says. "Nathan didn't lead us there. I even suggested we do it *tonight*, remember?" She hardens a little. "And you don't believe *I* would have led us there, do you?"

No. No, I don't. "Why didn't you just say? I would

have done anything for you." I'm so mad I'm on the verge of tears. "Anything."

"That's exactly the reason. I wanted it to be a friends thing. Before we all go our separate ways. I didn't want it to be a favour to me because my arm is broken or because of the car crash or because you'd 'do anything'. It's hard enough to be normal this month, isn't it? For anything to just be easy?"

I look at her. I look back at Nathan, who's smart enough to keep his mouth shut. Mel and Jared aren't saying a word either.

I remember what Jared said about me at his house. In this moment, he's never been more right.

I'm the one here who's least wanted.

Without another word, I put the car in gear and drive off down the road.

A few miles later, Nathan breaks the silence. "Don't I deserve an apology?"

I give him the finger and drive.

Chapter The Thirteenth, *in which the Prince is tricked into turning Satchel and second indie kid Finn over to the Empress of the Immortals; he tries to save them, but is forced to sacrifice Finn to do so; Satchel refuses to accept this and, through only her own cunning and bravery, thwarts the Empress; she saves Finn and as they flee, she steals a glimpse at the Immortal Crux, the source of the Immortals' power, through the Gateway; it is full of charms and jewels, with an empty space in exactly the shape of her amulet.*

◄O►

"So what were they, do you think?" Mel asks me, as she brushes our grandma's hair.

"More cops?" I shrug from the chair next to Grandma's bed. "More deer? I don't know."

"I wonder if we ever will."

"And if we do, I wonder if we'll regret it."

Our grandma leans against Mel's brush with her eyes closed, like Mary Magdalene when you scratch her between the ears. Mel's the only person she'll let do this. She never speaks while the brushing's happening, never mentions it when it's over, much less thanks her, but she'll sit still the whole time, enjoying it, quiet as a cat.

"No one died, though," I say. Mel shushes me and crooks her head to Mrs Richardson's empty bed. Someone did die. No idea how or when, but it must have been really recent, because they don't keep the beds empty here for long. Mrs Choi is still in the bed by the window. She must be sad for Mrs Richardson, because she barely waved when we came in. I lower my voice. "But that could just be because we're not indie kids. Or maybe it was just luck–"

"Do you *really* think Nathan has anything to do with it?" Mel asks. "Because I don't. And I think I'm a pretty good judge of people."

I sigh out through my nose. "Probably not."

"How much of this is jealousy?"

"Probably all of it."

Mel takes a final swipe with the brush. "You want me to plait it, Grandma?" Grandma says nothing, her head still back, her eyes still closed. Mel starts plaiting.

"So," she says, innocent in a way that I know something's coming. "You're going to start seeing someone?"

"Mom told you."

"Only to ask if I wanted to see someone, too. It was actually surprisingly supportive."

"I know. She's been different lately."

"I'll bet she feels like she's graduating, just like us, so she's finally noticing that the majority of her kids are leaving."

"Isn't it funny how we're not even pretending Mr Shurin has a chance?"

"He doesn't." Mel folds up one large plait, isn't happy with it, starts over. "Dr Luther again?"

Dr Luther was the psychiatrist I saw before, way back when. Mel saw her, too, and for those few times we went as a whole family, it was Dr Luther who tried to figure us out. This should be the place where I make fun of her, where I put her in my past as a goofy hippie-chick; a lonely lady, soft as a wild herb, looking at us poor, wounded kids with the eyes of a fawn.

Except she wasn't. She gave off this air of, like, total competence. Like you didn't have to worry she didn't understand you or that she didn't know what she was doing. Any idea how much of a relief that is?

"I think so," I say. "Time is short, and it's better than having to start from scratch."

"Time is short," Mel repeats. "It is, isn't it?"

It is. The Bolts of Fire concert is tomorrow. The prom is next week, then we graduate. Time is short.

Mel folds our grandma's hair between her hands in a twist I couldn't even begin to replicate. "Could you hand me that?" Mel nods at a bottle of old-fashioned anti-tangle cream my grandma used to like. I hand it to her. She squirts a bunch into her hand and massages it into Grandma's hair, filling the room with a really nice coconut smell.

Grandma suddenly laughs, the smell triggering something.

"What's funny, Grandma?" Mel says, smiling.

But our grandma just smiles back at her and then at me. "You remember the islands, Phillip?"

"Which islands?" I say. She doesn't answer, just closes her eyes, still smiling. "Was Grandma ever on islands?" I ask Mel.

"Vancouver Island, maybe," Mel says. "But I don't think Canada really grows coconuts." She finishes up with Grandma's hair, getting up from the bed and gently laying Grandma back down on her pillow. Grandma doesn't open her eyes again and is asleep almost immediately. The usual ritual after Mel does her hair.

Mel watches her, hands on her hips, brush in her hand. "She won't miss this when I leave. But that kind of makes me even sadder that I'll have to stop."

"I know," I say, standing, getting ready to go.

"Not yet," Mel says. I sit back down and she leans against the table by my grandma's bed. For a few minutes, we just watch my grandma and Mrs Choi sleep, that empty bed in the middle seeming like a hole either of them could fall into at any moment.

Mel's been spending a lot of time with Call Me Steve. She has also somehow managed not to tell our mother yet that Call Me Steve actually exists. She's afraid he'll become just another part of our mom's schedule, an issue to be dealt with, a point on a memo for her advisors. She's probably right. Mom's victory seems so assured, though, she's getting hardly any press coverage. They're concentrating on a nasty Senate race instead. My mom says this is the best thing that could happen, but I can also tell that the biggest deal in her life not being the biggest deal for everyone else is a little disappointing.

Mel picks up her bag and takes out a plastic container. She opens it.

I frown. "Is that your lunch?" We didn't eat together today. Mel was at the dentist getting a check-up on the enamel treatments she's been having to repair her teeth. But it wasn't a Novocaine-type thing and she could have eaten, *should* have eaten afterwards.

"Don't freak out," she says, but I'm already standing, already kind of freaking out.

"Mel–"

"Mikey, please–"

"You can't start again. It's bad enough me

doing it. I couldn't *take* losing you, Mel, I couldn't–"

She puts her hand on my mouth, rolling her eyes to our grandma, still sleeping.

"Mel," I whisper. And I'm nearly crying. I know what it's like to lose her, even for three or four minutes. It makes you live afraid every minute of every day that it's only a matter of time before it happens again. You can be happy. You can have fun. But it's always there. Always.

"I have moments, Mikey," she says. "You have 'em, too, I know, and mine aren't as bad as yours. But with everything that's been going on–"

"Is it Steve?" I say, suddenly ready to break him in half with my hands.

"*No,*" she says, firmly. "He's nothing like that at all." She sighs. "Though I did think about it. Like you would with anybody. Like you'd want to be sure you looked attractive enough for someone you really like, even if he doesn't care about that stuff."

"Mel–"

"Like your scar."

This stops me. She puts her hand up to it like Henna did, tracing it with her fingers. She drops her hand. "This is *my* scar. I carry it around. Most of the time, I don't even think about it."

"But sometimes you do."

"The world's uncertain, Mikey," she says, and then she repeats the words from earlier. "Time is short."

We look down at her lunch. It's a wrap, Japanese-style, salmon, shoots, rice. There's a fork tucked in next to it. Mel takes it out.

She hands it to me.

I don't say anything, just look at the fork, look at her, look at her eyes asking me a question.

"I'm going to be okay," she says. "I really am. Just do this for me today, yeah? Like old times. Remind me that it's possible to feel safe."

She's keeping her voice steady, but I can see the nervousness in her arms and shoulders. She didn't eat her lunch, and it's probably a bit more serious than she's letting on, but it's also probably a bit less serious than in my worst worries. None of which makes me feel any better.

"I would tell you if it was bad," she says. "I wouldn't tell Dad, I wouldn't tell Mom, I wouldn't tell Meredith. But I'd tell you. I promise."

"You promise?"

She smiles, and it's so true, my heart sort of hurts. "I really do, Mike. I don't want to die. I want to live. I want to live long enough so I can *really* live." She shrugs, and it's more relaxed, I can see. "Just a blip in the day. And I need a reminder."

I believe her. I know what a blip is. I think I'd know the look of someone who was having more than a blip that freaked her out. They'd look like me.

I get some salmon and rice on the fork. I lift it up.

And I feed her. Mrs Choi and our grandmother sleep, the room is quiet, that middle bed between them empty, empty, empty, and I feed my sister her lunch. We share our craziness, our neuroses, our little bit of screwed-up-ness that comes from our family. We share it. And it feels like love.

"I'm still mad," Henna says.

"Are you *sure* you want to do this?" I ask.

"Did you hear me? I said I'm still mad."

"Then you should be mad at yourself, because if

you'd told me it was you who wanted to paint the bridge–"

"And *yes*, I'm sure."

She *is* still mad at me. I'm kind of mad at her, too. But she called asking me to drive her here tonight, not Mel or Jared or *Nathan*. Me. And I said yes.

"Henna Silven…" The tattoo artist gives up even trying to pronounce her name from the list and just looks at her.

"Silvennoinen," Henna says. "It's Finnish."

"Sympathies," the tattoo artist says. "My last name's Thai. It's seven syllables long. You ready?"

"Yep," Henna says, standing.

She's eighteen. She doesn't need anyone's permission for this, though she had to prove it to the tattoo parlour receptionist guy when we came in the door. I'm still only seventeen, but that's okay, because I don't want a tattoo. Like really, really not.

"You're definitely sure about this?" I asked her a hundred times on the drive over. "You've never mentioned it before."

"I never nearly died before," is all she answered. She wouldn't tell me what she was planning on getting either. Or how she found this place. Or why we were waiting for this one particular tattoo guy to finish putting a hummingbird on a lady's upper boob. While we sat there, she did look through a catalogue of different types of lettering, so I'm guessing it must be words. She didn't tell me what words, though, because she was too busy saying she was mad at me.

"Hold on a sec," she says now, stopping me from following her in. I wait as she goes to the tattoo guy's chair – he's called Martin, which seems really old-fashioned for a cool Thai tattoo guy – and they have a quiet conversation about what she wants and where she wants it. It's going to be on her side, by her stomach, the side away from where the cast is now. She shows the tattoo guy a piece of paper she didn't show me. He nods, draws a few things on it, and I hear Henna say, "Exactly."

She gestures me over, making me sit on the other side from the tattoo so I won't be able to see it until it's done. Then she goes back to telling me how mad she is.

"You're too mean to him," she says, as Martin preps her, cleaning and lubricating the patch of skin.

Henna's so focused on me, it's like she gets tattoos every day.

"Your parents will go mental," I say, also not for the first time.

"My parents won't know. I'm not doing this for them."

"You really think they're not going to see it in Africa? You're never going to go swimming or sunbathing or–?"

Henna snorts. "You obviously know nothing about missionaries."

Martin the tattoo guy holds up his needle, ready to start. "You're going to Africa?"

"Central African Republic," Henna says.

"Isn't there a war happening there?"

"Yes," I say. "Her crazy parents are taking her anyway."

"I went through Tanzania, Malawi and Zambia two years ago," Martin says. "Most amazing thing I've ever done in my life."

"Were they shooting at you?" I say.

"Not really." Martin turns on the power to his needle. "Now, no one here is going to pretend this doesn't actually hurt, but it's a pain you'll find bearable, I promise."

"Thanks," Henna says. Then she looks up to me, eyes still annoyed, and holds out her non-cast hand across her chest for me to hold. I take it. She grunts slightly when Martin touches her with the needle, but she doesn't flinch. He paints in what must be a few dots, then asks, "How's that going to be? It won't get any worse, but it won't get any better, either."

"Compared to how much my arm hurt," Henna says, "this is like a mild headache."

"Good." Martin carries on with the tattooing.

"You know if your parents find out," I say, "they'll blame me and Mel for sending you off the rails."

"'Off the rails'?" Henna asks, wincing. "You talk like an old woman sometimes, Mike."

"I talk like a politician. My mom has a speech where she says 'off the rails' a lot when she's talking about the other party."

"Well, maybe it's time I went off the rails," Henna says, frowning. "Maybe I've been on the fucking rails for far too long."

"Language," Martin says, still tattooing. We both look at him. He's covered in tattoos, some of which aren't exactly family viewing. He sees us, shrugs. "Just a personal pet peeve. Everyone does it. So why be like everyone?"

He sticks her again with the needle. Henna tenses up. I think she's holding her breath. He finishes, looks up. "That's one element done." He re-inks his needle and gets to work on the rest.

"How many elements are there?" I ask Henna.

"Just never you mind," she says through gritted teeth. A single tear escapes from her eye. I wipe it away with my free hand. "Thanks," she says.

We don't say much through the rest of the tattoo. It takes a little over an hour, but from the area where I see Martin working, I don't think it's going to end up too big. A tattoo is out of character for Henna, which I think is her entire point, but a big, ugly tattoo and she'd stop being Henna altogether. It'll be something right-sized and good.

She looks down at it once, only once, during the whole procedure. "I didn't know they bled," she says.

"No one ever does," Martin says.

He finally finishes, gently pats the blood away, then covers it with a square of clingfilm, taping it to her body. "No swimming for a month," he says. "And try to keep it out of the sun for as long as you can."

"Do you have a mirror?" Henna asks.

Martin gets up and brings over a large mirror that reflects her side and the brand-new tattoo.

Under the cling film, her skin is livid from where it's been poked and written on. Blood wells up but not as much as I might have thought. The tattoo is there, clear as day, reflected in the mirror. It's just one word, in some really amazingly beautiful lettering. No wonder she wanted Martin specifically.

Henna takes my hand again. And she cries again. And I wipe away her tears again. "I don't even think your parents would mind if those were the rails you were coming off of," I say.

"I don't want them to know," she says. "This is mine. All mine."

In the mirror, reflected backwards, Henna now has a tattoo that reads, simply, *Teemu*.

oOo

I wake in the middle of the night for some reason or another. Maybe my own snoring was getting too loud or a dream I can't remember.

I say this because I know it's not the car that wakes me. I don't hear it until I've turned over and made myself comfortable again. A car not my family's is rare at our end of this very, very wooded road, but not impossible. There's a turning just before us and sometimes people miss it.

But then I realize it's heading in the wrong direction.

It's coming from the Field.

I get up without turning my light on and look out through my curtains. There's a car pulling slowly out of the entrance of the Field, like you have to do because of all the mud and bumps. It's got its headlights off and all I can make out are those small yellow lights on the side that some cars have for no apparent reason.

I don't know how many times I have to tell you that it's dark out here. We've got streetlights, but they're spaced far apart and the closest is down the road a bit, only enough to cast a shallow light as the car pulls out of the Field and past my driveway.

But it's enough to see the driver.

It's Nathan. He's been parked in the Field in the middle of the night, and now he's driving away with his lights off, hoping nobody sees him.

CHAPTER THE FOURTEENTH, *in which Satchel doubts the Prince's intentions towards her; he weeps, professing his eternal love, one that he's been waiting to give for millennia but had never found a repository for until he met Satchel; they kiss, it might lead to something, but then they hear the explosion from the outskirts of town.*

◄O►

"But you said you didn't want to go," Meredith says to our mom. "You said people took advantage of politicians in crowds and that it was like having squirrels crawl all over your naked skin."

"Try not to say that in public, sweetie," Mom says. "And while that may be true, Mommy's running for Congress now and to be seen at a Bolts of Fire charity concert in my own future district, hopefully–"

"But you said you didn't want to go," Meredith

says again, apparently too stunned to get past her main point.

"I didn't then, but I would like to go *now*."

Me and Mel wait behind Meredith. The concert's in an hour, pre-dusk so all the little kiddies get home in time for bed. Meredith is covered head-to-toe in Bolts of Fire fan gear: T-shirt, twisty bracelets, belt, shoe buckles, tasselled trousers like Sapphire wears in the "Bold Sapphire" video, a cowboy hat that has the clean-shaven Caucasian faces of Bolts of Fire around the brim.

"But you said–"

"Meredith," Mom warns. She looks at me and Mel. "I'm going to take her. Why is that a big deal?"

"It's a little out of the blue," Mel says, frowning. "Almost as if a campaign person heard you talking about it and suggested you go instead."

Mom's face hardens. "Neither of you even *like* this band. You're about eight years older than their target audience."

"And you're about *thirty* years too old," Mel says.

"There's nothing to discuss," our mom says briskly to Meredith. "I'm your mom. I'm taking you."

"But I've got three tickets," Meredith says.

"Even better. Do you want your brother or your sister to join us?"

Meredith looks back at both of us, looks at Mom, looks at both of us, looks at the floor, mumbles something.

"What was that?" our mom asks.

"I want them both," Meredith says, sticking her brave little face up into the air, her chin trembling a little. She's so freakin' brainy you sometimes forget that she's still only a kid.

"Well, you can't *have* them both–"

"I want them both," Meredith says, more strongly. "They both said they would take me. I got tickets for all of us. If you had wanted to come, I could have tried to get four, but you didn't. You said *you didn't want to come*–"

My mom's eyes flash. "There's always the possibility that no one gets to go."

"I thought this campaign wouldn't interfere with our lives," I said.

"When did I ever say that?"

"What about Ferocious Mama Bear?" Mel says.

"Did that mean you were just going to be ferocious to your kids?"

My mom throws her hands up. "I genuinely don't understand what the problem is–"

"They're *leaving*," Meredith nearly shouts. She's really crying now, her little arms crossed against her chest.

"Hey," I say to her, picking her up before my mom has a chance to. She's big, getting bigger, an unrecognizable teen before too long, but I can still lift her, even if it makes my still-tender ribs ache. She cries into my neck, the brim of her cowboy hat cutting into my ear.

My mom looks at the ceiling, hands on her hips. She taps her foot so fast Mary Magdalene comes running over and starts whapping at her shoelaces.

"Stop that," Mom says, under her breath. She looks at us. "Fine."

She leaves the kitchen. I can feel Meredith relax in my arms. "Good," I hear her say, her voice thick. "Can we leave now before she changes her mind again?"

o O o

"We're younger than every single parent," Mel says, looking around, "and older than every single fan."

The performance space at our pitifully small county fairgrounds is an outdoor amphitheatre, built next to a huge, sheet-metal stable where they have the livestock competitions during the fair. The biggest star that's ever performed here before now was a local girl who came third on a TV singing competition. Bolts of Fire are playing in the domed arena in the big city tomorrow night, where there'll be approximately eight million times as many fans.

We're about nine rows from the back, but the amphitheatre is so small and deep – dug partially into the ground – that there really isn't a bad seat. There are actually fewer parents than I expected, though it's also possible they're commiserating with each other at the coffee bars before the actual music starts. Mostly it's just little girls. More than you've ever seen. More than you would think could possibly fit into a small county fair amphitheatre. So many it's like space and time folded together and every little girl who ever lived will arrive eventually.

"Do you see any of your friends?" I ask Meredith.

"Bonnie isn't coming," she answers. Bonnie is the other girl in her grade who takes all the insane extra tutoring that Meredith does. They have Jazz & Tap together. Bonnie's mom is the meanest person I've ever met in my entire life.

"Anyone else?"

Meredith doesn't say anything, just keeps looking around. I begin to wonder if there *is* anyone for Meredith besides Bonnie. God, poor Meredith.

"You don't have to sing along," Meredith tells us, "but I'm going to. Just don't make fun of anything."

"We won't, Merde Breath," Mel says.

"And don't call me that."

"Where's the cancer girl?" I say, trying to see if they've roped off a VIP pit somewhere down front.

"She's called Carly," Meredith informs me, very seriously. "Our Thoughts and Prayers are with her."

"I heard these tickets were going for $3,000 on the internet," I say.

"NO TRUE FAN WOULD DO THAT!" Meredith yells. "And it was fan-club members only and you had to *prove* that you lived here and everyone had to show ID at the gate."

She has a point there. It was like getting on an international flight with the President just to get inside. And that was *after* the half-hour it took to get through the rows and rows and rows of TV newsvans and journalists covering the story. We kept hearing reporters say "this little middle of nowhere" as we passed. Which, yeah, I also say a lot, but it's different when I say it.

"Anyone want a pop or something?" Mel asks.

"No!" Meredith says, horrified. "It's going to start in five minutes."

"Oh, please," Mel says, "concerts never start on–"

"Ladies and Gentlemen!" the loudspeakers announce. *"Please take your seats, as the Bolts of Fire concert will start in FIVE minutes!"*

There's a deafening scream from around the amphitheatre that happens at about the height of my ribcage. Little girls jump up and down and hug each other and go crazy and are just otherwise disturbingly hysterical, while their parents start streaming in from the side, holding, yep, cups of coffee – no alcohol for adult prisoners of Bolts of Fire.

"That's it?" Mel asks, having to shout over the whoops and hollers. "A five-minute announcement?

No opening act? No music and lights to warm up the crowd?"

"If the crowd were any warmer," I shout back, "we'd need paramedics."

Somehow a group of voices singing "Bold Sapphire" has emerged from the sound avalanche, and more and more of the girl crowd join in, including Meredith. *"I broke Bold Sapphire's heart on the day she turned eighteen/I never meant to do it and I hope she still loves me."* Within seconds, the amphitheatre is one loud, off-key, but really enthusiastic voice singing the band's biggest hit.

Which, I admit, is kinda catchy.

"Are you *singing*?" Mel says to me, eyes wide.

"No," I say, too fast.

The amphitheatre lights go down, which is ridiculous as it's still daylight, but never mind, eighteen hundred little girls burst into simultaneous overwhelmed tears. I think my eardrums are about to explode. Meredith, though, is practically levitating. She's between me and Mel and she's so excited she doesn't know whether to hold our hands or clasp her own or just stand there and hyperventilate. She tries to do all three, which basically makes her like every girl here.

She looks up at me, tears in her eyes. "I'm so happy."

"They're not even on yet."

She just cries some more.

The screams get even louder as someone comes onstage, but they drop respectfully quickly as we all see it's a girl in a big-deal hospital wheelchair being brought on by what I'm guessing is her mother and a nurse. The girl's got an oxygen tank with her and looks really bad. The non-nurse/possible mother takes the microphone that's centre stage.

"Hi, everyone," she says, "I'm Carly's mom."

There's another huge scream.

"Thank you," she says. "Carly has something she'd like to say to you."

The audience quiets down. Every girl there is pulled as taut as a bow to listen to Carly. I hear a girl behind me say, mournfully, "I wish *I* had cancer."

Carly's mom brings the microphone over to Carly. We can hear her ragged breathing for several beats before she says anything.

"Yikes," Mel mouths to me with a sad look.

"Would you..." Carly says. Breath, breath. "Please..." Breath, breath. "Welcome..." Breath, breath. "Bolts..."

That's all she gets out because the audience screams like they're watching their families be murdered in front of them.

Bolts of Fire are walking onstage.

There are five of them, they've got names, I could probably tell you what they are if I search my memory, but how can it matter? The noise in here is so bad my phone is vibrating even though it's not ringing. Mel has her fingers firmly in her ears, and I can see a father in the row in front of us sympathetically pointing to the earplugs he's wearing.

The Bolts of Fire guys – all in fashionable stubble with fashionable lopsided hair that manages to weirdly suggest that they're both thirty years old and fifteen years old *at the same time* – bask in the applause for a minute, then gesture for the audience to quiet down. This takes awhile, and even then it's only relatively. The dark-haired one who does most of the singing talks anyway.

"Thank you all so much!" he says.

Another skull-fracturing roar.

"Ready for a good time, people of–" and then he names, not our little town, but the larger town about an hour away. The audience roars anyway. Mel shoots me an irritated look, but I can't hear a word she says.

"We're here today," says the blond one who doesn't sing very much but who's prettier than the others, "for one special Bolts of Fire fan."

Another roar as they put a Bolts of Fire cowboy hat on Carly's head.

"We're going to start," says the one whose voice you can always tell is modified by computer to make him hit the right notes, "with Carly's favourite song."

"Maybe you know this one," says the main singer.

He sings an "oooh" and holds it, the others joining in one at a time. I look at Meredith. She's pretty much tearing her shirt in ecstatic weeping. I put an arm around her and she leans into me, holding on like I'm comforting her at a funeral.

Then Bolts of Fire, all together, a cappella, surrounding poor Carly in her wheelchair: *"I broke Bold Sapphire's heart on the day she turned eighteen…"*

And the scream from the crowd is so loud that it takes a second before we realize that a bomb has gone off.

At first, we all assume it's some kind of bizarrely timed firework from behind the stage, but then pieces of stage set and burning curtain come flying straight at us, Bolts of Fire have been knocked to the ground, and Carly's mom and nurse have wrapped themselves around Carly's body to protect her.

As the debris starts falling – fortunately it seems to be mostly styrofoam and cheap fabric – the screaming of the audience changes so much you can feel it in your body, a rising terror that seems to come out of the ground like a flood of water, rising up to choke you before you even start to swim.

We are in the most incredible danger.

I pick Meredith up immediately, knocking her hat to the floor. She's so scared, she doesn't even mention it. I'm so scared, I don't even notice my ribs. Mel presses herself against us, arms wrapping around me and Meredith.

"What was that?!?" Mel screams.

"We've got to get out of here!" I scream back.

"They're coming!" Meredith yells and we turn down to the rows in front of us.

A tidal wave of panicked parents and panicked little girls is flowing over the seats up the wall of the amphitheatre.

Coming right at us.

There's no time to even think. I turn with Meredith in my arms, and we run. I climb up over row after row, the seats above us quickly vacating, thank God. Mel is behind us, shielding Meredith from any more debris. I see a few bloody faces as we rush on and I can only wonder if there's anyone really badly hurt, but there's no time for that as I keep climbing.

We get stuck behind a frantic mom, trying to herd three girls in front of her. Without breaking stride, Mel picks one of the girls up. The mom, with what seems to be superhuman strength, picks up the other two and we all climb together, as that's still faster than the clogged aisles. We're lucky by a factor of a thousand that the biggest exits are at the back of the amphitheatre, wide staircases heading down into the green fields of the fairgrounds. Me and Mel and the woman reach the top of one and scramble down the steps, only just barely able to stay standing in the rush of people.

"There!" Mel yells and starts heading towards a bit of the fairgrounds that have been left wooded, with a clearing in the middle for picnics and barbecues. Most of the crowd pour out past the confused news crews to the parking lot, but we swerve to the side with some others, finally stopping in the trees, huddling together. Mel puts down the girl she picked up and the mom hugs her in with the other two, saying, "Thank you thank you thank you thank you," to Mel.

I set Meredith down, and she instantly throws up. My adrenaline is so high my hands are shaking uncontrollably, but I do my best to rub her on the back. "It's okay, Meredith, we're out and we're going home right now."

"Mikey," Mel says. "Look."

Hovering over the amphitheatre, against the now-setting sun, a pillar of blue light is disappearing from where the explosion was.

"It wasn't a bomb," Mel says. "It was them. Whoever the hell *they* are."

In the past, there's been collateral damage from whatever the indie kids are involved in. But it's hard to think of "collateral damage" when it's me and Mel and freakin' *Meredith* and almost two thousand little girls.

Whatever it is has just gotten worse. A lot, lot worse.

"Aren't you Alice Mitchell's daughter?" we hear.

Cynthia, the bitter little blogger who's always attacking my mother and who tried to drag Mel's past into the press conference, is standing in the clearing, pad in her hand, filming us. "You are, aren't you? The anorexic one."

Another camera crew from the big city affiliate has seen her and is rushing over to us as well, trying to find someone who'll tell them what happened.

"Where's your mother?" Cynthia sneers at my sister. "Why isn't she here to protect her children?"

Mel barely hesitates. She steps forward, snatches the pad out of Cynthia's hands, and punches her right across the face.

CHAPTER THE FIFTEENTH, *in which the Prince explains to Satchel that the Immortal Crux, which allows passage between worlds, depends on the amulets; the one she wears is missing from it, and though it protects her, its absence is causing holes to rip in the boundaries between the Immortals' world and hers; the life force – "you would see it as a kind of blue light, but it would burn you, Satchel, it would burn you right through" – is spilling out and causing damage, including the accident at the amphitheatre which killed Satchel's friend Madison; "Should I give it back?" Satchel asks, wanting to save lives, but giving it back would fully power the Immortal Crux and only make the march of the Immortals into her world unstoppable; it's an impossible dilemma.*

◄O►

The police are saying a gas main exploded.

A gas main.

The only person who died was an indie kid called

Madison who was in Calc with me and Jared. I spoke to her a bunch of times in class. She was definitely not stupid, but they say she was smoking outside the amphitheatre after dropping off her sister at the concert and it ignited a leaky gas main.

Bullshit.

First of all, why does a teeny tiny amphitheatre in the middle of a field at the state's smallest county fair have a gas main running right behind its only stage?

Second of all, Madison used an inhaler so totally didn't smoke.

Third of all, bull and shit.

Lots of people were hurt, including Bolts of Fire – so the rest of the entire *world* hates our little town now – plus Carly's mom and nurse. No one very badly, though. Four of five Bolts of Fire still performed "bravely" the next night in the big city while the blond one got his front teeth replaced. Carly didn't get hurt at all, which is one small blessing. One *very* small blessing if that's all you've got when you have terminal cancer and the concert of your dreams is blown up.

Meredith got treated for shock at the scene by Call Me Steve, who was the first person Mel phoned. He showed up in an ambulance, saw to Meredith, kissed Mel really hard, then ran off to help other people.

I like him.

Our mom just cried. Genuinely, I'll give her that, and for all of us, too, not just Meredith. "That someone could do this," she choked out, in front of a bunch of journalists when people still thought it was a bomb, "in a place where *my* children are..."

But she hugged us. I thought she'd never stop. "You're *sure* you're not hurt. You're *sure*?"

"Just a little freaked out," Mel said. "More than a little, actually."

And our mom hugged us again. She didn't even yell at us for not letting her come along to the concert to be exploded herself.

Quite a few news crews ended up getting footage of Mel attacking Cynthia. So far, it's actually *helped* my mom's campaign. "I thought it was a terrorist attack," Mel told the cameras, keeping a straight face that I'll remember with joy until I die. "And suddenly here was someone identifying me as a politician's daughter. I thought I was a target, so I protected my younger brother and sister."

There will be no charges filed, not even for the pad Cynthia was using, which Mel, perhaps unnecessarily, broke in two by stomping on it. Cynthia blogged about it all. I don't think anyone cared.

"Bet that was pretty awful, huh, Merde Breath?" Jared says, squeezing the life out of her, her little bare feet a metre off the ground.

"Uh-huh," Meredith says, muffled, into his neck. "And don't call me that."

He sets her down, hands on her shoulders, and looks her in the eye. They just stare at each other for a minute, then she smiles. "Your hands are getting hot," she says. "But I'm okay."

He smiles back at her. "You sure?"

She nods. "But show me the lights anyway."

He checks to make sure my parents aren't watching – which is for show, as we all know they're both out of the house or he wouldn't even be here – then pulls his hands slightly away, casting a light down her arms from the palms of his hands. She giggles and throws her arms around his enormous legs in a last hug. She's slept in Mel's bed the past two nights since the explosion. I can't blame her, and I don't think Mel's in any hurry to get her out either. None of us have been back to school yet, but I think today is pushing it. It's not actually that much fun missing school when there's so little of it left.

"Did you actually do anything for her?" I ask, as Meredith heads into the kitchen to make herself a snack, always keeping us in sight.

"I don't know," Jared says. "I was feeling all these good things for her, all my hopes that she wasn't hurt." He flexes his hands. "Maybe some of that got into her."

"Are you getting more powerful?" I ask. "Is that … something that would even happen?"

He just frowns and flops down on the sofa. Mary Magdalene sits on the arm of it, watching him, purring and kneading her paws into the fabric. "You take good care of Meredith, okay?" Jared whispers to her, touching her lightly on the nose. The cat immediately jumps off the couch and starts following Meredith around the kitchen.

"Gas main, huh?" he says to me.

"Don't get me started," I say, sitting down next to him. "The question is, what are we going to do about it?"

"What *can* we do about it? We don't know what's going on."

"Come on, Jared, surely the Gods must know something–"

"Mikey, it doesn't *work* like that. Don't you think I'd be finding out if I could?"

"Finding out what?" Meredith says, scooching up on the couch next to Jared with a plate of cheese and crackers, Mary Magdalene sitting firmly on her feet.

"Finding out what's really going on, Bite Size," Jared says, not lying to her either.

Meredith nods seriously. "There's still hardly anything on the internet. Rumours and theories and indie kids disappearing, but mostly it's just people monstering other people for thinking it's vampires again or for *not* thinking it's vampires again. Everyone thinks they know better. Everyone." She eats a cracker. "I think I'm going to give away all my Bolts of Fire stuff."

"I think I'd want to, too," Jared says.

o O o

"You're sure *you're* okay?" he asks me later, driving us to work after Mel came home from her day out with Call Me Steve. I could have called in sick, but I was getting antsy just sitting around the house. It felt like I was waiting for something to happen. Which has to be the worst part of being young. So many of your decisions aren't yours; they're made by other people. Sometimes they're made *badly* by other people. Sometimes they're made by other people who have no idea what the consequences of those decisions might be. The bastards.

"I'm fine," I say.

"You're not."

"I spent an hour brushing my teeth this morning because every time felt like I hadn't done it right. Mel finally noticed and got me out of it."

"See?"

"Jared, we have to *do* something. Make the indie kids tell us what they know. Or *Nathan*–"

"Jesus, Mike, would you leave him alone? I told you, he was with me and Henna at the movies."

"He could still have some part in it. I don't trust

him. Why was he in the Field that time? What's he doing hanging around my house in the dark?"

"His mom is like the saddest person in the world. I told him we hung around the Field, so maybe he just needed a place to get away. You're getting obsessive."

"Of course I am! Have you *met* me? They could have killed my sisters, Jared. It could have happened right there in front of me."

"And you," Jared says, more softly. "They could have killed you, too."

I look at him, then back out the windshield of his tiny car. "Thanks, man."

"Look, what do we know?" he says. "We know that only one person died."

"An indie kid."

"Yes, an indie kid. A nice one. Who was smart and good at math. She didn't deserve that. None of them did."

"Unless they're the ones who stirred all this up."

"Even then," Jared says, sternly. "And come on, have you seen them lately? They're even more scared than the rest of us. And with good reason."

I don't say anything, but he's probably right about that.

"And what I *did* find out from my grandmother—"

"You talked to your grandmother? I thought she was off in her realms, unreachable."

"It wasn't easy, in fact it was a huge giant pain in my ass, but what I did find out is that, when it happened before — because she was there once, remember? — this kind of big public thing meant the beginning of the end."

I wait for him to continue. "What end?"

He shrugs. "However it's going to be solved. However the indie kids are going to solve it."

"*If* they solve it."

"They always have."

"Doesn't mean they always will. Doesn't mean people won't get hurt before they do. Doesn't mean more people won't *die*."

Jared pulls into a spot in the Grillers parking lot. "We may never find out what's actually going on, Mike. It may all end with us not seeing anything else—"

"But Jared—"

"*Listen to me,*" he says, sounding angry. "We've got prom, we've got graduation, we've got the summer. Then everything changes. Are you going to live all that time until we go afraid?"

"Probably."

"Please don't." He's still weirdly angry. "Not everyone *has* to be the Chosen One. Not everyone has to be the guy who saves the world. Most people just have to live their lives the best they can, doing the things that are great for *them*, having great friends, trying to make their lives better, loving people properly. All the while knowing that the world makes no sense but trying to find a way to be happy anyway."

He's gripping the steering wheel, hard, and I can see light flashing from his palms. "What aren't you telling me?" I ask. "What's going on?"

He just sighs and the light dims. "I don't know what's going on. I don't know about the cops or the pillars of light or what the indie kids have got themselves mixed up in, but I do know this: one, they better not blow up the high school before we graduate, and two" – he holds up his palms again, they flash a little with faint light – "if anyone I care about is put in harm's way again, there's going to be holy hell to pay. Literally."

And that makes me feel a little bit better.

Our shift is crazy. Tina has to be out on the floor full-time, waiting tables herself, even on what should be a slow week night. It's like the town knows something's happening and doesn't want to be alone either. Mel and Henna bring in Meredith, who sits in my section this time. I take them enough cheesy toast to feed a cheesy-toast-loving sperm whale.

"How's the tat?" I ask Henna, who answers by hugging me.

"It itches," she says in my ear, then she leans back and looks at me.

"What?" I ask.

"Just you. Saving people."

"So you're not mad at me any more?"

"Who cares about mad?" she says.

"No Nathan tonight?" I can't help myself from asking.

She frowns and slides in next to Meredith, who's

already got cheesy-toast butter on her face. We're so busy, that's all I can really talk to them right then. I bring cheeseburgers for Henna and Meredith and a chicken salad for Mel, who digs in like she's famished. I notice slightly too long. She makes a face.

They're still there half an hour later when something completely unexpected happens for the second time this week. It's not a bomb this time, even if it might as well be.

My dad shows up.

"Dad?" I say, so surprised I stop right there, at the entrance where Tina is wrangling with menus and trying to seat people. There's a line of customers waiting to get in, which usually only happens on Sunday mornings after all the churches let out. My dad's at the front of the line, looking around, slightly stunned, but not smelling of booze that I can tell.

"Busy tonight, huh?" he says.

"What are you doing here?"

He fingers his collar, only catching my eye in brief little glances. "Meeting your mother. Is she here?"

"You're meeting her *here*? At the restaurant?"

My surprise must finally sink in because he stops,

seeming confused. "I think so," he says, and it's almost a question.

"Uh," I say, because I really don't know what else to say.

Tina finally can't take it any more. "Are you busy?" she says to me, eyes wide, voice high. "Because I am!"

I snap out of it. "Dad, Mel and Meredith are sitting over there with Henna." I point. Three astonished, frozen faces stare back at us from their booth. "Why don't you ... you know ... sit with them?"

My dad nods, but doesn't head over to the booth. "Can I talk to you for a sec?" he asks me.

Without even looking at her, I hand the coffee pots I'm holding to a really-very-angry-now Tina and follow my dad out into the parking lot. It's only just getting dark. The rain let off the week before the Bolts of Fire concert and you can tell that summer might actually be on the way. If we live to see it.

My dad scrunches up his face like his mind's elsewhere and pulls again at his collar. "Why don't you take your tie off?" I ask.

"Hmm?" he says. He doesn't touch the tie. He looks at the moon, up already, only about half-full.

"When I was your age, we really did think we'd be living up there by now."

I wait. He doesn't continue. "I'm kinda busy, Dad. What's up?"

He scratches his ear. I think for a second that he's not steady on his feet, but then I realize he's just shuffling around, not staying still. I lean in and smell him again. He gives me a small grin. "Nope," he says. "Sober."

"Well," I say. "That's good."

"Listen," he starts, but again doesn't finish.

"Dad, seriously, I–"

"I'm going to go into rehab."

He stops because a family has come out of the restaurant. Tina leans out the door behind them, looking at me with furious eyes. I flash a "one minute" index finger at her and she goes back inside.

"That's, um," I say, "that's *great*, Dad. I–"

"Not until after the election. But I'm going to go."

I frown. "I think you're a bit more important than–"

"Not her idea. Though she's been asking for years, hasn't she?"

"I wouldn't know, Dad, but even so, I think she'd probably–"

"Don't want to ruin her big moment." He fidgets some more, catching my eye and looking away. I lean closer.

"Dad? *Dad*. Look at me."

He hesitates, then looks at me full on. Even in the dusk, I can see that his pupils are pretty much the size of dinner plates. "What have you taken? Valium? Something prescription?"

"I'm fine," he says, straightening up. "I've just got to make it to the election and then I'll go into rehab and we'll all be a family again."

"I'll be living two states away."

He slumps a bit. "Yeah. Yeah, I knew that."

"What are you doing here, Dad? Are you really meeting Mom or did you drag me out of the busiest night of the year just so you could tell me you're going to rehab in six months?"

He frowns again, looking back up at the moon. "There were going to be cities up there. No poverty, no war. That's how it was supposed to be."

"Okay, I've got to go. I'll get Mel to drive you home—"

"I need to borrow some money," he blurts out.

Well, *that* stops me. "You what?"

He sighs. "The campaign didn't think it was a good idea for me to have full access to the accounts." He shrugs, like he can't blame them. "I'm short of cash. I don't want to ask your mother."

I don't know what to say. What *can* I say? I'm not even angry at him. Just so sad I can barely look him in the face.

I take out every tip I've collected that evening and hand him the whole wad of cash.

"Thanks–"

"Go wait in your car," I interrupt, still not looking at him. "Do *not* drive it."

I turn my back on him.

As my dad lurches into the parking lot, I step into the entryway of the restaurant, grabbing the front door handle. A small red light catches the corner of my eye. I look over. Behind some bushes, in the shadows–

Nathan, smoking.

"I'm sorry," he says, quickly. "I saw you talking to him and I was going to say hello but then…"

He doesn't finish, but I know. He was going to say

hello, but then he heard my dad being embarrassing and tragic and he got stuck there, not wanting to alert us to his presence by going either backward or forward.

"How much did you hear?" I say, heat in my voice.

"Mike, I–"

"I can't believe you smoke," I say. "It's disgusting. It stinks. You get breath like a dog. *And* it won't kill you fast enough."

"It was an accident, Mike, I swear."

My chest is burning, like it's being squeezed in a molten vice. "I've got to get back to work."

I don't look at him once the rest of the night, even though he sits with Henna after Mel takes Meredith and my dad home. At the waitress station, Tina uses every opportunity to shout at me, but I don't listen to her. I'm too busy repeatedly counting ketchup bottles and wishing I was dead, wishing I was dead, wishing I was dead, wishing I was dead.

CHAPTER THE SIXTEENTH, *in which Satchel cries in her room, taking the blame for all her friends' deaths, even though everyone she knows assures her that it's not her fault; Dylan knocks on her window; he comforts her, finally kissing her; she stops him, says she understands his desire for her, but she'll have to break his heart; they're surprised by a knock at the front door; her mother yells up that it's second indie kid Finn; Dylan looks surprisingly serious, and asks, "How do we know we can trust him?"*

<o>

"Hey, Dr Luther."

"It's good to see you again, Michael."

"Is it? Doesn't that mean you failed last time, though?"

"Still concerned about failure, I see."

"I know, I know. 'Why does everything have to be something you win or lose?'"

"*Do* you know?"

"I thought I did."

"…I should tell you up front that your mom's been talking to me."

"As a patient?"

"No, but don't sound so shocked. She's been talking to me as your mother. As your *concerned* mother. She told me things have been … challenging for you lately. It's only fair that you know that. I won't, of course, tell her anything that we discuss here, though. That's between us."

"Did she tell you she's campaigning again?"

"She did. How do you feel about that?"

"It's weird."

"How so?"

"It's like it doesn't have anything to do with me this time. Like our lives have already separated and this is something that's happening to her rather than to us. Plus, she's being okay about it, actually."

"That's a generous thing for you to say."

"It's true. Mel's been kept out of it except for at the concert. Did you see that?"

"I did."

"That was so great. *She* was so great. She couldn't have done *that* last time."

"That's good to hear. There was always a lot of strength in your sister. But we're not talking about her, are we?"

"No. I guess we're not."

"Tell me what's been happening, Michael. Tell me why you've come back to see me."

"I thought my mom already told you."

"I want to hear it from you."

"...I've been getting ... stuck. In loops. Again. Like I can't leave the house unless I lock the door a certain way but I don't really know what that certain way is or how there are even supposed to be different ways to lock a front door. It happens a lot when I'm washing myself, too, if I don't do it in just the right order. Or if I start to touch things and count them, I can just get ... stuck there."

"What do you think will happen if you don't do these things?"

"I don't know. Something awful. Something I won't be able to handle. Everything will fall apart."

"Everything?"

"I don't know."

"Is it something to do with the spate of deaths at your school?"

"What do you know about those?"

"They're not unknown. They've happened before. It's one of the more terrible sociological phenomena."

"Do you know what's causing them?"

"'Cause'? They were accidents and suicides, as far as I understand. Is there an underlying cause?"

"No. No, I guess not."

"Unless you mean it's something like the vampires or the soul-eating ghosts. Don't look so surprised. We had armies of the undead when I was your age. It was pretty awful and scary, but it *was* confined, kept quiet, involving a fairly small group of people while the adult world looked on obliviously."

"...I don't know what to say about any of that."

"Does this time around have anything to do with you?"

"I'm not an indie kid."

"No."

"But we were at the concert. And Henna and I hit those deer. And ... other stuff."

"That I probably wouldn't believe? Even after what I've said?"

"Maybe."

"Well, I don't need to. As long as you do, it's an important thing to talk about."

"Jared said we can't all be the Chosen One. In fact, hardly any of us can."

"Jared is still your best friend?"

"You've got a good memory."

"I take good notes."

"Yeah, my best friend. He looks after me. He saves me from these loops sometimes. He's more than my best friend, really."

"You love him."

"Yeah, but not like that, I don't think. He's gay, but it's different. It's like he's my family, except better, because I've chosen him."

"I understand. He's important for your feeling of safety in the world."

"Well, *yeah*. And I ... I don't know what I'm

going to do when everything changes."

"Graduating, you mean?"

"And going off to college. It's not just Jared. Mel's going across the country, we're leaving Meredith on her own…"

"These are normal fears. It would be unusual if you *didn't* feel them."

"Yeah, but…"

"…but?"

"I don't know if I'm going to make it."

"Make it how? Michael?"

"You're the only person who calls me Michael."

"Make it how?"

"…Um."

"It's okay."

"It's not, though."

"I mean, you're safe here. If you need to cry, you can."

"It's not okay."

"How is it not?"

"…They don't need me."

"Not like you need them."

"No. Jared said he thought I always made myself

the least-wanted person in the group, but he told me that wasn't true."

"You didn't believe him."

"If you have to have someone tell it to you, how can it be true? How can you not just be the damaged one who needs reassurance all the time?"

"Don't we all need reassurance? Aren't we all damaged in some way?"

"You don't understand."

"Then help me. I want to."

"Look, it's… They've all got other lives. Jared's got all this family stuff, Mel's dating a doctor, Henna's going to *Africa*. And what do I have? I have *them*. I don't have anything else."

"And that makes you feel like you matter the least."

"Yeah. And I'm in these loops and I'm trapped and I can *feel* that I'm trapped and getting out of them is as simple as just *doing something else*. Anything. But it's getting harder and harder to get out of them myself and what if I go away and start a new life and I get trapped in one and I can't get out of it?"

"Okay, what if that does happen?"

"…"

"Michael?"

"…I can't say it. It's embarrassing."

"I am impossible to embarrass."

"…"

"Tell me, Michael. What if you get trapped in a loop and can't get out?"

"…I'll kill myself."

"That's a very final choice."

"It's better than being afraid forever. It's better than always being afraid."

"Those are the only alternatives? Being afraid or being gone?"

"That's what it feels like. And I don't know what to do."

"About what?"

"About *everything*."

"Isn't that the problem, though? Isn't that what's causing the fear? Why do you have to solve everything? Why can't you just solve today?"

"I can't even do that!"

"You can and you have. You're facing one of the biggest life changes anyone ever has to face: leaving school and going out on your own. Yet you've survived a car accident that you might not have *and* helped your badly hurt friend. You suffered a traumatic event at that concert, but look how you acted in saving your little sister."

"Mom told you all that."

"She thinks very highly of you, Michael. She worries about you."

"Then she should tell me. Please don't defend her."

"All right. I'm just saying that you *have* solved a lot. You feel like you can't face anything, that it'll crush you, but you're *here*. In this room. All those things you're facing, and you still said to someone – said to your mother, no less, who I know you don't regard as a natural ally – that you needed help. Doesn't that sound like someone who's looking for solutions?"

"...Maybe."

"I'm going to ask you a question. What if everything *did* fall apart? What then?"

"I don't understand."

"If you didn't do these things, if you stepped out of the loop before finishing it the 'right' way, what would happen? Would you survive it?"

"I don't *know*. That's kind of the whole deal."

"Let me ask the question another way, then. Haven't you *already* survived everything falling apart?"

"...what?"

"Melinda nearly died."

"She *did* die."

"Either way, if that's not everything falling apart, then what is?"

"I don't want it to happen again, though."

"You said yourself she was doing great."

"But Meredith is–"

"You're responsible for Meredith, too? Everything fell apart at that concert and you all survived *that*. If I were to ask Melinda whether you were the least wanted, I doubt she'd answer like you have. Meredith, too, and I would bet money that your friend Jared would say the same."

"They're just being nice."

"All of them? All the time?"

"Because I'm the broken one."

"Is that true? Is that *really* true? You said they all have other stuff to deal with. I know exactly the difficulties your sister has faced, for example–"

"Yeah, but… She's doing better now."

"Perfectly?"

"Well. No."

"But you're measuring yourself against her?"

"Why are you coming at me so much?"

"I'm sorry. I don't mean to. I'm only trying to say that there might be other ways of looking at things. Ways that don't make you so afraid. Ways that don't make you wish you were dead."

"…"

"Do you cry a lot when you're on your own?"

"Almost never."

"Then obviously you need to, Michael. It's okay. There are some tissues there if you need them."

"…I feel like I'm at the bottom of a well. I feel like I'm way down this deep, deep hole and I'm looking up and all there is is this little dot of light and I have to shout at the top of my lungs for anyone to hear me and even when I do, I say the wrong thing or they don't really listen or they're just humouring me."

"Because they couldn't possibly care about you."

"…It's hard to feel that. They tell me. They *show* me. And I still don't feel it."

"Why do you think that is?"

"The fear gets in the way. And I get stuck in a loop."

"Because if you can just get the loop *right*–"

"*Yes*. If I can just get it right, it'll all be okay. I'll, I don't know, save everyone. And the world won't fall apart. And it's getting harder to do."

"I bet it is. All the stuff that's going on for you."

"All the stuff that will always go on."

"That's probably true, too."

"Can I tell you something, Dr Luther?"

"Yes."

"You won't laugh?"

"I won't."

"...I hate myself. I feel like an *idiot* saying it because, blah, blah, teen angst, boo hoo, but I do. I hate myself. Almost all the time. I try not to tell anyone because I don't want to burden them, but I feel like I'm falling farther and farther away from them. Like the well's getting deeper and I'm running out of energy to climb it and any minute now, any *second*, it's going to stop being worth even trying."

"I won't keep harping on this, but I will say again,

just gently, because it's true. You're here. And that's trying."

"…Can you help me?"

"Yes. For now, as a start, I'd like to put you on some medication. Why are you making that face?"

"Medication."

"Medication … is a failure?"

"The biggest one. Like I'm so broken, I need medical help."

"Cancer patients don't call chemotherapy a failure. Diabetics don't call insulin a failure."

"This is different and you know it."

"I *don't* know it. Why is it different?"

"Because it means I'm crazy. Crazy is different."

"Michael, do you think cancer is a moral failing?"

"What kind of cancer?"

"Don't play. You know what I mean. Do you think a woman who gets ovarian cancer is morally responsible for it?"

"No."

"Do you think a child born with spina bifida or cerebral palsy or muscular dystrophy is at fault for their condition?"

"No, but–"

"Then why in heaven's name are you responsible for your anxiety?"

"…Because… What?"

"Why are you responsible for your anxiety?"

"Because it's a feeling. Not a tumour."

"Are you sure?"

"You think I have a *tumour*?"

"No, no, no, no, no, no. Not what I meant. A feeling is pride in your sister. A feeling is fear at the concert that makes you act. A feeling is embarrassment or shame. A feeling may or may not be true, but you still feel it."

"And anxiety is a tumour on your feelings?"

"Feelings don't try to kill you, even the painful ones. Anxiety is a feeling grown too large. A feeling grown aggressive and dangerous. You're responsible for its consequences, you're responsible for *treating* it. But Michael, you're not responsible for causing it. You're not morally at fault for it. No more than you would be for a tumour."

"You realize I'm now going to obsess about having a tumour."

"I'm sorry. Ill-chosen words. But if you're going to obsess about something, obsess about your obsession being a treatable disorder. Obsess about it not being a failure of something you've done or something you didn't do or some intrinsic value as a person that you fail to have. Medication will address the anxiety, not get rid of it, but reduce it to a manageable level, maybe even the same level as other people so that – and here's the key thing – we can talk about it. Make it something you can live with. You still have work to do, but the medication lets you stay alive long enough to *do* that work."

"..."

"Michael?"

"..."

"Isn't it possible to think of this as a success?"

"I never wanted to go back on it."

"You told me, just now, just *today*, that you'd rather be dead than have to go through this much longer. I take that seriously. I don't think your suffering is fake. I don't think these feelings about wanting it to end are fake. I don't think your self-hatred is fake. So why do *you* think it's fake?"

"I don't."

"Don't you? Doesn't a part of you think you're making a big deal out of not very much? That if you were somehow not so weak, you could be happy and free just like everyone else?"

"...Kind of."

"You came to me because you wanted my help, yes?"

"Yes."

"Then here's my help. One, your anxiety is a genuine and very painful problem, not one you're making up. Two, you're not morally responsible for causing it. It's nothing you did or failed to do that makes it happen. Three, medication will help treat it, so that four, you and I can talk about ways to help make life bearable, even liveable."

"Will I have to be on it forever?"

"Not if you don't want to. The decisions are entirely yours."

"...I hate myself, Dr Luther."

"But not so much that you didn't come asking for help."

CHAPTER THE SEVENTEENTH, *in which Satchel doesn't know who to trust, so she follows her police officer uncle to see if she can find the source of the blue energy on her own; she enters the basement of the high school while the prom – which Satchel is completely not interested in except in an ironic way – is going on above; while the music plays and people dance, she stops her uncle from opening a fissure that will swallow the whole gym and everyone in it; she knocks off his unattached head in the process and the blue light fades from his body; she weeps at her actions and bravery, but the Prince arrives, terrified, saying they have to run, as fast as possible.*

◄〇►

"You look amazing," I tell Henna at her door on the night of the prom.

"Thanks," she says, shyly. "I kind of *know* I look amazing. How weird is that?"

Her dress is, I guess, custard and burgundy, but that

really doesn't begin to describe it. Most prom dresses I've seen are either puffy to the point of cloudiness or cut so short and sheer you keep wondering if the girl is cold.

But Henna.

There are no gimmicks with her dress, but then there never are with her. She isn't trying to be ridiculously fashionable but she's not ridiculously *old*-fashioned either. She looks like a grown-up, that's what it is. A really beautiful, beautiful, serious and beautiful grown-up. Even the cast on her arm looks like she got it from lifting a car off a refugee child.

"You look … amazing," I say again. "I mean it."

"You're not so bad yourself."

I'm just in a tux.

But, okay, maybe I do look good in a tux.

"Very handsome," her father says, coming up behind Henna with her mother.

"Hello, Mike," her mother says. She holds up her phone. "Picture?"

"Yeah," I say, and Henna slides up next to me while her mom snaps us. We look for all the world like we're going to the prom as dates. Which is what her mom and dad think. They also think she's staying over with just Mel out at the cabin as a kind of we've-almost-graduated treat. They have to know Henna's not that boring, don't they? They must know that the rest of us are going out there, too, and maybe just this once they're overlooking it? Or maybe in Finland this is perfectly normal, even for the devout.

"Have a good time," her mom says, kissing her on the cheek. Her dad does the same. They've always been this formal, like royalty. Solemn in a way that makes everyone else feel slightly ridiculous. They stand together, his arm around her shoulders, watching Henna take me by the elbow and walk down to the waiting limousine.

"Oh, my God," Henna says, seeing it.

"I know."

The limousine turned out to not quite be what we ordered. Those were "all out", it seems, to other prom nights, maybe even at our own school. So despite a regular black limo being available when we made the booking and paid the non-refundable deposit, that's not what showed up at my house to pick up me and Mel. I texted the others to warn them, but that still doesn't prepare you for seeing it in person.

It's a Hummer limousine. A *yellow* Hummer limousine.

"It's horrible," Henna says admiringly. "So horrible it's kind of wonderful."

"I told you."

Mel leans out its open door. "At the very least," she says, "you feel safe in it."

And we do. This is probably how tanks feel. We pick up Jared next (Mr Shurin, horrified: "How much gas mileage does this thing get?") then, because everyone else wants it, Nathan. ("You can't smoke in here," I say before he even sits down.)

Call Me Steve declined a limo pick-up ("Already feel weird going to a prom seven years after I graduated," he told Mel. "And so you should," Mel told him back, "but you're coming anyway.") He's at the school, waiting for us, opening the door so Mel can get out first. He pins on her corsage – as the only couple officially on a date tonight, he's the only one who thought of buying one – and says, "This vehicle is a crime."

"Against nature?" Mel asks.

"Against judgement," he says. "Against taste. Against good sense. Against the planet…"

They walk off towards our high school gym arm in arm, still smiling, still talking about the wonderfully horrible Hummer limo that's already gathering a small crowd of other arriving couples.

Jared, huge in a tuxedo slightly too small, says, "Don't we all look amazing?"

"Yes," Henna says. "Yes, we do."

The theme of our prom is "Forever Young".

I know.

We can't afford to have it in a hotel in the big city, which is what most schools do, so we're stuck with it at our own gym. Usually you have a formal dinner beforehand with your dates, but as Grillers is the nicest restaurant in our little town, we decided to just skip that. Mr Shurin says he's stocked up a bunch of food at the lake, so as long as that hasn't been eaten by otters or marmots or bears, we'll be fine.

"Dance," Henna commands, taking me by the elbow again.

"Me first?" I say, following her out to the dance floor. It's a slow dance, so I put my hands on her hips and she rests the non-cast hand on my shoulder.

"I'll dance with Nathan," she says. "I'll dance with whoever I like."

"But what about the desire in your stomach? That you can't help whenever you see him?"

"If you'd have ever shut up about him, maybe you and I would have got together by now."

"In the spirit of exploration?"

She leans in, puts her head on my chest. I feel her sigh. "I wonder if realizing you're not sure about stuff is what makes you a grown-up?"

"Lots of adults seem *really* sure about things."

"Maybe they're not grown-up either."

"Tell that to my mother."

"Tell that to *mine*."

We dance. It's nice.

"Just think," Jared says, handing me a cup of punch. Yep, punch. In a cup. "This could be our last party without alcohol ever."

"We're not twenty-one for three more years," I say. I look around to Henna, now fast-dancing with Nathan in a group with Mel and Call Me Steve. "And none of us are exactly big drinkers."

"More a metaphor for making our own choices," Jared says. "And why *don't* any of us drink?" Then he glances at me, thinking of my father and the rehab story. "Oh. Sorry."

I shrug and drink my punch.

"How's the medication going?" he asks me, lowering his voice.

I shrug again. "Takes a while to work. And there's a lot of talking to Dr Luther that goes along with it. Feeling okay, though."

"That's good," he says.

"Do you like yourself, Jared?"

He looks at me, surprised. I know he guesses exactly why I'm asking. "Sometimes," he says. "Sometimes not."

"Sometimes not," I repeat. "Those things going on. Those things you can't talk about."

Jared turns to me. "We haven't danced enough."

"...Together?"

"*All* of us together." He cocks his head to our friends, dancing in the crowd, smiling, working up a sweat, laughing, dancing like fools. The hall is packed now, probably for the same reason as the restaurant: people know something's going on and just want to be together.

I have a flash of terror that this would be a great opportunity to blow a whole lot of people up again. If there are any *gas mains* running below the school, that is–

"What is it?" Jared asks.

"What if we're in danger here?" I say, feeling my chest contract, feeling suddenly desperate, like I need to find a loop, quickly, one that will save us all from being blown up.

"Do you see any indie kids?" Jared asks. I look around. He's right. There's not one.

Which makes me sort of sad, really.

"We'll be fine," he says, dragging me out onto the dance floor.

"Maybe we should check outside," I say, but my words are lost in the volume of the music and the crush of people suddenly around us. We join

Henna, Mel, Steve and Nathan. And we dance.

It's nice, too.

"We're going to take off," Mel says, about an hour later. We're all standing in the rest area, where the school have put out a bunch of couches just slightly too brightly lit to encourage heavy kissing. "We'll meet you at the cabin."

"Now you're *sure* we're not going to be ritualistically murdered?" Call Me Steve says, actually looking a bit nervous. "Prom night. Group of diverse teens. Remote cabin…"

Mel blinks. "Are you being *serious*?"

"I'm a doctor. We see stuff. There've been strange things going down."

We all just stare at him.

"What?"

"That's not the story that's happening," Mel says to him. "We're not the kind of people that story happens to."

"What? I don't…"

She kisses him. "I love that you're worried," she

says, "but you're worried about the wrong things."

"I..." is all he says because she's already dragging him away. She waves goodbye. Call Me Steve is driving her to our place. They're going to change, then she'll get the clothes we all packed and bring his car and hers out to the cabin, so we've got an extra there after the Hummer drops the rest of us off. Jared and his dad left Jared's car out there today, too. It's a whole plan.

"You guys ready to go?" I ask Henna and Jared.

"I think I'm done," Henna says. "My arm is starting to hurt from all my phenomenal choreography." She looks to the dance floor. "Nathan's still out there, though."

And he is, just kind of dancing on his own with a cup of punch. (Seriously, a cup of punch; it's embarrassing.) I guess he's making one of those memories to take with him.

"Okay," Jared says, "one more dance for me and then we'll go. I'll find you guys."

He presses back out onto the dance floor. Henna and I find a couch. We're surrounded by people taking pictures of each other with their phones and then sending those pictures to a person ten feet away and then everyone commenting on them. This makes perfect sense to me.

"You having a good time?" I ask.

"Yeah," she smiles. "I really am. Who knew it'd be this much fun?"

"I'm starving, though."

"Oh, God, me, too. I hope Mr Shurin brought out some steaks–"

She stops because she's seen Tony Kim. He's coming over to us. I feel her immediately soften.

"Hey, Henna," he says.

She gets a really tender smile on her face. "Hey, Tony."

I know Tony came to the prom with Vanessa Wright, the ex of mine and the girl who I lost my (and her) virginity with, but he's not with her right now. It's kind of a shock to see him. He really dropped away after Henna broke up with him.

"Long time no see," I say.

"Hey, Mike," he says, his face tight. I know how it must look, me here with Henna on this couch. He must have known – since everybody does – how much I've mooned after Henna all these years. And here we are, together, at prom. Looking like dates. Part of me actually wants to explain that, no, really, I have no idea what's going on with me and Henna, that I think she's still after this Nathan guy, that I'm even more confused now than ever, that Henna herself probably doesn't even know how she feels and from what she's told me, she's kind of okay with not knowing right now.

I don't say any of that, though.

"You look incredible," Tony says to her.

"Thanks," she says, warmly. "You look great, too."

This is true. Tony is stupidly handsome but not in an arrogant way. He was always a nice guy. Always good with Henna and to her. They were really beautiful together. Even now, because I can see how hurt he still is without her.

Well, *tough*, though. Right?

"So," he says, sticking his hands in his pockets, looking a little uncomfortable. "Prom, eh?"

"Yeah," Henna says.

He looks over to me but doesn't say anything.

"We're not here together," Henna says, maybe a little too firmly. "I mean, we *are*, but we came as a group. Mike and his sister. Jared."

Tony nods. "Saw you guys dancing."

"Where's Vanessa?" I ask. Everyone frowns at me for this.

"Getting a drink," Tony says, looking around as if he could see her. "I think. Listen, Henna—"

"Tony—"

"I just wanted to—"

"I can't do this, Tony."

"I just want to call you sometime," he gets out. "Just to talk. That's all. No pressure, nothing. I just... I miss you."

Henna bites her lower lip. "I miss you, too, Tony."

He smiles, really sadly.

"It'd be great if you called me," Henna says. "Before I go to Africa. That'd be great."

He nods. "See you," he says, shuffling away.

Henna watches him go. "Poor guy."

"I guess so," I say, a little too hard.

"For someone I've never dated," Henna says,

rising, "you feel entitled to *way* too much jealousy."

I have to rush after her to catch up.

The Hummer waits for us. Our driver is called Antonio, and he opens the doors while we're on our way over. Henna and I get in and wait for Jared and Nathan, still dancing inside.

"I'm sorry," I say.

"It's okay," Henna says, leaning against me in the giant Hummer seat. "Actually, it was pretty nice having everyone think you were my date."

"Yeah."

She puts her arm through mine. "So why don't we just say that you were?"

"What about Nathan?"

She looks up at me. She smiles, then shakes her head.

"What?" I say.

But then she's looking past me, out the open door. I assume it's Jared and Nathan coming, but she points to the far exit of the gym where the dance is being held.

A door is open in the dark. A girl I recognize from school whose name I can't remember comes out, crying. A boy I've never seen before has his arm around her, comforting her.

Blue light flickers in the doorway behind them, then vanishes.

"They're not in prom clothes," Henna says.

"You know what?" I say, getting out of the seat. "I'm going to go find out what the hell is going on–"

"Mike, don't–"

"Where are you going?" Jared says, showing up with Nathan and accidentally blocking the exit.

"To talk to them," I say, looking over his shoulder.

But when we turn to look, they're gone.

"I think I want to get out of here, Mike," Henna says, pulling at my arm, getting me back in my seat. "I think I really do."

And I can't argue with her.

I never could.

CHAPTER THE EIGHTEENTH, *in which Satchel flees with the Prince, thinking it's to safety, but the Prince has betrayed her; he takes her to the Court of the Immortals, which has been searching for the perfect Vessel for their Empress, a better body for her to inhabit forever; that body will be Satchel's, made ready by the amulet left not by indie kid Kerouac, but by the Prince; the Empress says, "I sent a Messenger to make your world ready for us. It took several tries before one survived what the process required"; the Messenger reveals himself; it's been Dylan since the night he first came to her house; he begins the ceremony that will kill Satchel and allow the Empress to live in Satchel's body; fissures open all over town to allow the invasion of the Immortals to begin.*

◄O►

"There's a smell," Nathan says, entering the cabin.

"Otter," Jared says. "Sorry."

Nathan winces. "No, I didn't mean... It's not a *bad* smell–"

"Just musky," Mel says, handing everyone a beer, which Mr Shurin stocked up for us. I know that lots of children of alcoholics become alcoholics themselves and maybe that'll happen one day to me or Mel, but we kind of figure with her eating issues and my anxiety issues, we're already covered. (We hope for the best with Meredith, like we do with everything else.) I wasn't kidding before, though; none of us really like to drink all that much.

Except Nathan, it turns out. He downs his beer in one like it's a challenge, does that end-of-drinking gasp, and reaches for another. He sees us all staring at him. "What?" he says. "Oh." He takes the second one and sips it.

"Music?" Mel says, taking a phone out of her bag and plugging it in. Tunes start to play, quietly, not dancy, just good stuff. The cabin has a small main room with a sofa and a little kitchen. There are two tiny bedrooms, which means at least some of us are going to have to sleep on the couch. I already assume one of them's me.

"What is there to do up here?" Nathan asks. "Not being a dick, just genuinely wondering."

"Eat, for one thing," Jared says, opening the fridge.

"Oh, God bless you, Mr Shurin," Henna says, next to him, taking out some steaks.

Call Me Steve and Jared end up doing the cooking. The rest of us change out of our formal wear. Everyone but Nathan switches to soft drinks. None of us has eaten for about eight hours and the steaks smell so ridiculously good, we hover in the main room like incredibly serious hyenas. "I will start gnawing on your shoulder if this takes much longer, Jared," Henna says. "I'm not kidding."

"Ask and ye shall receive," says Steve, dishing up a bunch of plates. I should probably stop calling him Call Me.

The dinner is, in its own way, better than anything we'd have got in a restaurant. Mr Shurin is so awesome he remembered everything: steak sauce, napkins, salt and pepper. Even salad and salad dressing.

"I wish he was *our* dad," I say.

"You get who you get," Mel says.

PATRICK NESS

"I didn't mean it like that."

"I know."

There's a TV in the cabin, though it's so old it's not even flat. Hooked up to it is – are you ready for this? – a VCR. An actual VCR that you put cassettes into. I'm pretty sure you can't even buy those any more. There are a few cassettes at the cabin, too, all of which I remember from when I started coming out here to the cabin with Jared as a kid.

"We've got *Pretty Woman*," Nathan reads, drinking another beer. "Or *Tremors*."

"*Tremors*," five of us say at once.

So for a while, it's just steaks and *Tremors*. The sound of people eating and the sound of people being eaten.

Who'd have thought that would actually sound sort of happy?

"Are you kidding me?" Call Me … um, just plain old *Steve* says, when Jared comes out of one of the bedrooms in his swimsuit.

"It's almost summer," Jared says, smiling.

"It's May," says Steve. "At night. And that lake is fed by a glacier."

"It's June tomorrow, and I've been swimming in that lake my entire life, Doc," Jared says. "Who's with me?"

"I'm not allowed yet," Henna says, patting her tattoo.

"You're also wearing a cast," I say.

Henna looks at her arm, almost in surprise. "I've gotten so used to it, I forget it's there." Her eyes widen. "I'm going to have to walk down the graduation aisle with it."

"I'm up for a swim," Mel says, standing.

"Are you sure?" Steve says. "You don't really have the body fat." There's an awkward pause at this. Steve back-pedals. "I'm just speaking *medically*–"

"That's okay," Mel says. "It's sweet. You can apologize by getting in the lake."

"I didn't bring a swimsuit."

"Oh, we don't wear suits in the lake," Jared says, mischievously. "This is just for show."

"It's dark," Mel says. "You'll be fine."

"Seriously?" Steve says.

"I'll come, too," I say.

"And me," says Nathan, but he wobbles a little bit and has to sit back down.

"I don't think so," Jared says, in a way that Nathan doesn't disagree with.

We head out to the water's edge, even the non-swimmers. There are a few other cabins along the shore, but ours is the only one with a light on. It's a bit early in the season, and even that word, "season", isn't quite right. These are cabins for people who probably can't make it out on a Friday night to begin with because they're working late to pay for the cabin they can't quite afford. Mr Shurin inherited his from his father, but even then, it hasn't had a new paint job in my lifetime.

Nathan and Henna sit on a log, huddling next to each other, even though it really isn't cold out here. He even puts his arm around her.

"Quit staring," Jared says, dragging me down to the little dock that serves this cabin and a bunch of others. He's the first one in, shucking off his swimsuit and jumping into the black water in a cannonball of his big, hairy body. The splash hits us on the dock and is unbelievably cold. Jared pops up, gasping. "Now, *that* will wake you up."

I take off my clothes and jump in next, keeping my back to my sister and Steve to give us all some privacy. The water is a shock, it's true, but not as bad as I was fearing. I surface and start to freestyle swim out a ways to warm myself up. By the time I swim back in, Steve and Mel are in the water, Steve not too happily.

"My family is from Honduras!" he shouts. "Where the ocean is *warm*!"

"Have you ever been to Honduras?" Mel asks him, her teeth chattering.

Steve smiles. "Shut up."

I swim over to where Jared is treading water. He's watching Nathan and Henna. They're just leaning against each other, talking, lit up by the single outside light from Mr Shurin's cabin. "Hey, Henna!" Jared calls. "Turn off the light. Let's just have the light of the moon!"

"Ooh, good idea," she says, leaving Nathan on the log by himself.

"Thanks," I say to Jared.

He looks a little surprised. "For what?"

The light goes off and the effect is sort of incredible. The sky is clear aside from just the fewest clouds lingering around the summit of the big Mountain. Otherwise it's just the moon, not even full, but when that's all there is, nothing else competing with it, it's bright enough that our heads cast shadows on the water.

"I think I've endured enough fun," we hear Steve say, and he climbs back up on the dock. His body is a little heavy but almost completely hairless. He's got a little paunch that I bet he'll never get rid of. It makes him seem like the most normal guy in the world. I kind of love him for it. He wraps a towel around himself quickly, then holds one open for Mel to step into as she gets out of the water, too.

"*Is* this an endurance test?" I say to Jared. He smiles and splashes me with his hands. I'm enjoying it, but I can already feel how I won't be in five minutes. I start to swim back to the dock to get out. That's when Nathan stands up from the log.

"Look!" he says, pointing beyond us, across the lake back in the direction of town. We see the reflection even before we turn.

There are flashes and streaks of blue light criss-crossing the sky, fast, frantic, like a lightning storm, over our town. We can't see the town itself, only the trees that line the lake, but even at this distance, which is at least seven or eight miles, the sky above where we just were is like a town-sized fireworks display.

"My parents are okay," Henna says, hanging up her phone. "They want me to come home, though."

"Is that when you said, *There's no way in hell*?" Mel asks.

"Yes. Yes, it was."

Meredith is in the capital with our mom, who had to be down there for campaign stuff in the morning and wasn't – this is how much we've abandoned hope for my dad – going to leave her with just him to watch her. Meredith answered on the first ring anyway, having seen video and feeds of it online. "It's only small towns," she said. "Remote ones like ours, but they're all calling it 'freak lightning'."

"As long as you're okay, Meredith," I said to her.

"I am," she said. "Are you?"

I don't really know the answer to that question. We're all gathered along the waterfront, just watching the lights. They've been arcing for a good half-hour now. We haven't heard any sirens. Mr Shurin, at his house, says he hasn't heard anything either, though there are a lot of people who've pulled their cars over just to watch it. Steve called the hospital, and they told him they didn't need him. So whatever's going on is at least not killing anyone.

Or not killing anyone that we know of, that is. I wonder how the indie kids are doing?

"Is it the end of the world?" Nathan asks.

"I doubt the end of the world would start with our town," Jared says. "Though maybe it would, actually."

And then all the lights stop.

"Whoa," Nathan says, pretty drunk by now.

The lights weren't making any sound, not any that made it this far out to the lake at any rate, but it still feels like a silence has fallen. We all stare at the empty sky for a few quiet minutes. Then Mel stands, taking Steve by the hand. She leans under his arm as they head back into the cabin.

"I'm ready for bed, too," Henna says, getting up from the log. Nathan gets up with her, more than a little stumbling. "You all right?" Henna asks him.

"Yeah," he laughs, "just a little hammered."

"We noticed," I say, still sitting next to Jared. "All of us." Jared elbows me, hard.

Nathan just stares at me. "You don't even know me," he says. "You haven't even tried."

"No," Henna says, taking him by the arm and leading him to the cabin. "No, he hasn't."

I watch them go until it's just me and Jared out here, him sipping a beer, me having a Coke. The smell of the beer is making me a bit grumpy, too. The staler it gets, the more it smells like my dad.

"You need to lay off him," Jared says.

"Why? We don't know anything about him. He said he used to be an indie kid; what if he brought all this shit with him?"

"Mike–"

"And why was he by my house? Why did he want to get up on that bridge?"

"That was Henna's idea–"

"He could be the cause of all this, for all we know.

And now he's in there with *her*."

"She's not going to sleep with him," Jared says, frustrated. "He's not going to sleep with *her*."

"How do *you* know?"

And there's a silence. I turn to him.

Then something clicks.

"Oh, no. No way."

"Mike, I–"

"Jared, please don't say–"

But then he stands, his attention suddenly grabbed by something out in the darkness. He's still in his towel. So am I, with just my jacket over me. His eyes are running back and forth across the undeveloped part of the lake down from the cabin. It's full of trees.

There's a blue light among them. Getting closer.

"Shit," I say, standing, too, ready to get the others, ready to run–

"No," Jared says. "No, it's not…"

He takes off. *Towards* it. "Jared!" I yell.

But then of course I run after him. My feet are bare and I'm stepping on rocks and pine cones and God knows what else in the dark. "What are you doing?!"

The blue light emerges from the line of trees, and I see.

It's a mountain lion. I'd wondered why none had come to pay homage to Jared since we've been at the cabin, but I thought maybe he'd asked them to leave him be tonight. But here comes one, running in an odd, crooked way, its eyes glowing blue and an aura of blue light around it.

"Jared, don't!" I say, still ten steps behind him. "The deer were–"

But he and the mountain lion have met. It drops at his feet, flopping over them, looking up at him through the blue glaze. He kneels at once, putting his hands on it. I reach them.

"Jesus," I say.

The mountain lion is horribly mangled. It's hard to even look at.

"Was it hit by a car?" I ask. I step a bit closer and the blue light flashes out, catching my forearm. It's like being hit with boiling water. I yell and jump back. A ton of it is hitting Jared, but he's not moving, must be a God thing. But if that's what's hitting the poor mountain lion...

Oh, man.

Jared says nothing, just concentrates hard on the big cat. Then he lets out a grunt and the blue light vanishes. In the sudden darkness, I can't see him at first, just hear the mountain lion yowling, obviously in terrible pain.

"It's all right, girl," Jared whispers, and the palms of his hands light up. He presses them against her, and her whimpers lessen. I go closer now. The blue light seems to have blasted through her over and over again, erupting from inside her at different points. The tears and burns against her beautiful tan fur are painful to even see.

"Just be still," Jared keeps whispering. "You're safe here. You've found me."

She grows even quieter, until it's just her breath we hear. She's curled up against his leg, like she was seeking refuge in him. Which I guess she was.

"I can't save her," Jared says to me, his throat heavy. "She ran all this way to find me, getting mangled the entire way, and I can't save her. It's beyond the reach of my powers." He holds her against his shins, gently stroking her. She sounds ragged, but at least no longer in pain. He leans down close. "You rest now. You sleep, without pain, in the arms of your God."

Her breathing slows, then slows again. I wait there with them both until she makes no more sounds at all. "Dammit," I hear Jared whisper, and even in the moonlight, I can see the tears on his face. He strokes her sadly a last time, then lays her head down on the grass.

"Are you okay?" I ask, stupidly.

"The indie kids think they're the only people in the world," he says. "They think their actions don't affect anyone but them."

"I know. The whole world is like that."

"Not everyone," he says, looking over at me. "Not you."

"Jared–"

"I'm in love with Nathan," he says. "And I think he's in love with me."

"Yeah..." I say. "I kinda figured that out just now."

"I'm sorry I didn't tell you. At first it was too private, too fragile, and he's still freaked out about liking guys and..."

He doesn't finish, but I can guess. "You've been lonely."

He just nods. "I didn't want to harm anything. I didn't want to bring it out into the open and have the light kill it somehow. And I couldn't stand the thought of hurting you."

"It doesn't," I say.

"You're my best friend, Mike. The best friend I've ever had. You've never judged me, you've taken every weird thing I've thrown your way completely in stride, you never ask for much in return even when I'm dying to give it. You didn't even let your mom and my dad get in the way of us being friends."

"I wouldn't have let this get in the way. I wouldn't have been hurt. I'd have been happy for you."

"You hate Nathan."

"Because of Henna's stomach feeling for him—" I stop. "She knows, doesn't she?"

"Yes."

"Does everyone?"

"Yes."

"Oh."

"Mike—"

"No. No, I, um…"

I don't know what to say. Because *this* is what hurts me.

Henna's on the couch when we make our way back to the cabin. I walk ahead of Jared, not looking back. He and Nathan will share the other bedroom, I guess, though I doubt anything will happen. Jared's never going to be the guy who takes advantage of a drunk person.

"Night," he says when we get back inside.

"Night," I say. After a beat, he goes into one of the bedrooms.

"Hey," Henna says from the couch. When I don't answer, she sits up. "You okay?"

"I don't think I am."

She opens her arms. I lay down next to her, and she holds me. It's the closest we've ever been, but all I want her to do is just hold me.

CHAPTER THE NINETEENTH, *in which Satchel escapes the ceremony in the nick of time, aided by the sudden appearance of second indie kid Finn, who she realizes is the only one who truly cares about her; they run, but the process of the Immortals taking over the world has begun; then Satchel, through only her own cleverness, figures out how to close a fissure using the amulet; but there are so many, all over town, will she be able to close them all before the Immortals take over completely?; as they rush to close a fissure in Satchel's own house, Dylan the Messenger steps through; Satchel and second indie kid Finn are forced to kill him; she weeps, Finn holds her.*

◄O►

Back when I first went to the hospital on the night of the accident, Steve gave me this oil to put on my scar to keep it from stretching and getting bigger. I often get caught in a loop with it, rubbing it in, wiping it off, rubbing it in, wiping it off, until I'm sure I'm doing far more stretching damage to the scar than would have ever happened by just normally using my face.

But this time I actually stop myself. I rub it in and leave it. I wait to see how that feels. But no, I'm not trapped. I can *see* the trap. I can see it waiting for me to step into, if I want, see the spiral just there, ahead of me, waiting. But I can also wash my hands and dry them and leave the little bathroom at the cabin.

The medication must be working, because that's what I do, after taking one last long look at my scar.

"I'm sorry," Mel says.

"I don't want to talk about it," I say.

"I wanted him to tell you. He kept saying he would–"

"It's fine. There's nothing to talk about."

I go to the dock, strip to my underpants and jump in the lake again. The sun's up. It's morning. The water's still ridiculously cold. I go down deep and just hover there. Rays of sun stab down at me through the surface. They don't make me any warmer.

Henna filled me in on some of the details. Nathan hung around outside Grillers to meet Jared on his breaks. Nathan was in the Field that night because he met Jared there after a fight with his mother. Henna was at home with her parents on the night of the Bolts of Fire concert because Nathan was with just Jared at the movies. All those mysterious Saturday nights that Jared's been taking? Whatever they were before, they've been something different lately.

Everyone could see it. Except me. Because I was too focused on Henna.

And is that my fault? I'm asking seriously. If I'd been looking at my best friend in the world and not myself or the girl that I claim so hard to be in love with, then maybe I'd have seen it, too. Because I guess it was obvious.

But what were they waiting for? Why were they waiting at all?

Are we all friends or are *they* just friends?

You *always* *think* *you're* *the* *least-wanted*, Jared said.

Sucks to be right.

I surface before my lungs explode. Henna's waiting on the end of the dock. "Wanna drive me back?" she asks.

I look up at her from the water. "No," I say.

She waits.

"Yes," I say.

"I thought you'd figure it out," Henna says, as we drive. "It was a surprise to me, too, but eventually I realized I was getting no vibes off Nathan at all, no matter how strongly *I* felt. And then I'd see him looking at Jared a little too long."

"I don't..." I say. "I didn't... Jared's always been secretive."

I said goodbye to everyone, even Nathan, wincing through his hangover, and Jared, who kept his distance, waiting for me to come closer. But I left instead.

"This is stupid," I say, feeling my chest get tight,

like I'm going to cry. I cried during the night when we lay on the couch together. She let me. And even though she didn't tell me about Jared and Nathan before either, I'm not mad at her.

I just feel so dumb.

"You guys don't have to treat me like I'm going to break," I say. "Everyone does. Mikey with the OCD. Mikey with the medication now–"

"We never did, Mike–"

"Mel *died*. She's still weird around food and everyone treats her the same. Like they should. *I* do. I spend a lot of time doing that."

"Jared is a quarter *God*, Mike. And I've got freak parents who are taking me to a war to talk about Jesus and feet. Everyone's got something. Not even just us, everyone we know." She looks thoughtful. "Except maybe the indie kids. They're probably the most normal ones out there."

"I wonder what was going on last night. With the lights."

She shrugs. "Probably some apocalypse."

"I feel so stupid," I say. "Just so, so stupid. Right in front of my face. And no one tells me."

"If it helps," she says, "it means I really was your date to prom."

I drive some more. I don't say out loud whether it helps or not.

My mom hands me an envelope as I walk in the door. "I checked," she says. "You aced them."

Our finals results. I open it. I did ace them, even Calc. College was kind of a formality – I knew I wasn't going to fail – but it's nice to have the formality all wrapped up. New life, here I come, I guess.

"You're back early," my mom says, going to the kitchen.

I follow her. "So are you."

"Meredith made me." She smiles, but I know it's true. "That freak lightning storm."

She says it in a way that's almost asking me about it. "I don't know either," I say. "I don't know a lot of things."

"You know enough to go to a good school." She takes some drinks out of the fridge, not even asking what I want, just somehow knowing that I'd love a cream soda. "You know enough to face a future with some confidence."

"Do I?"

"I'm proud of you. I'm proud of your sister, too."

"How'd she do?"

She grins, pouring me my soda. "It's like you're twins sometimes."

"Good," I say. "Good."

She hands me my drink. We just stand there for a minute, drinking, like it's the most normal thing in the world. "I really am proud of you, you know," she says, then she gets a tough look. "I want a world where you can live and be happy."

"That'd be nice," I say, but she doesn't seem to hear me.

"I've gotten it wrong in the past. Really wrong. I haven't even managed to get you guys to believe in my political party." I open my mouth to object, but she stops me. "Don't deny it. I don't even care. All I care about is keeping trying. To make the world safer for you and your sisters. Any way I know how." She takes a drink. "I've seen things you wouldn't believe, Mike."

"You said that before. What kind of things?"

"Things that would keep you awake at night. Things that would make you desperate to try and protect your own kids." I see her look past me. "Hey, sweetheart."

Meredith's come in, holding her pad. She looks worried.

"What's wrong?" my mom asks.

Meredith turns her pad to show us.

"I didn't know!" Jared says. "I swear it."

"Your dad sure as hell knew!"

"And I'm as pissed off at him as you are!"

"*Are* you? It's my *sister*!"

Mr Shurin's campaign got hold of Cynthia the blogger. The story was pretty much dead, gone, Mel a hero, my mom the mother of a brave daughter. But now the footage of Mel punching Cynthia has been recovered from her destroyed pad (recovery paid for by Mr Shurin's party). Unlike all the news cameras who turned to us too late, this is footage that shows Mel having a bit more time to recognize the woman, more clearly decide to punch her, and then a great big shot of Mel's foot stomping on the pad.

It's all been put up on Mr Shurin's website along with photos of Cynthia looking like she's fallen off a cliff face-first. Mr Shurin's campaign site has big ol' headlines on it: "Questions asked about brutal attack by Alice Mitchell's daughter!" "Political blogger says First Amendment rights breached, will sue!"

Because yeah, she's suing us, too.

Jared didn't answer his phone as I drove over and wasn't at his house when I got there. I had to wait for him to show up from the drive back from the cabin with Nathan. I barely let them get out of the car.

"She's my friend, too," Jared says.

"Really?" I'm shouting a lot. "Like you're *my* friend?"

"That's... Shit, Mike–"

"I thought your dad was a good guy–"

"He *is* a good guy. I'm sure there's an explanation–"

"I don't *want* an explanation! I want him to lose like the loser he always is!"

Jared's face gets harder. "Watch it," he says, quietly.

"Watch what? What are you going to do?"

Nathan's standing off to one side, still hangover-squinting. He says, "I'm sure this can all be straightened out–"

"Shut up!" I shout at him. "Things were fine around here until you showed up."

"Christ sake, Mike," Jared says. "Is that was this is about? I *knew* I couldn't tell you! I *knew* you'd be jealous!"

"Jealous?" Nathan asks.

But Jared's still going. "You stick to me like a tick! I can't breathe without you wanting to know it! I can't live my life without you wanting to crowd in."

"You never tell me anything, Jared! It's always the same. All this stuff you don't want me to know! Like some power trip you have to have over me at all times."

And then he says–

Well, he says this:

"Maybe if you were a *real* friend instead of an endless bag of need, I'd have told you about Nathan *first*. Did you ever think of that?"

At that, I just stand there.

And stand there some more.

Jared's face softens. "Mike–"

"Just get your dad to take it down," I say, looking at the ground.

"Mike, please, I didn't–"

"Get him to take it down."

"I will."

I get in my car. They watch me go.

"But I'm *not* worried," Mel says, as we sit on her bed.

"Are you sure?" I ask her.

"It's politics," Mel says, leaning back with a frown. "It's filthy and it's disgusting and dirties everything it touches." She shrugs, still frowning. "It'll blow over in a week."

"Mom went mental," I say. "She's already got lawyers on it. There's no way that lady wasn't made-up in those photos."

"They don't want me, they want Mom. So it's her problem. I told her that and she agreed. She says she's fixing it." She hugs herself, lightly. "I'm just … really disappointed about Mr Shurin."

"I *know*–"

"Maybe even nice guys get tired of losing."

I feel an ache in my stomach when she says the word "losing". *I want him to lose like the loser he always is*, I said to Jared. About his own dad.

But so what? He attacked my sister.

Almost like my thoughts summoned him, both of our phones buzz at once. It's from Jared. *He's taking it down. Today. Says the campaign team kept pushing him on it and he finally said yes and regrets it. He's pulling out of the race altogether. I'm sorry. I didn't know.*

"Wow," Mel says, quietly.

"Won't stop the blogger suing, though," I say. "The damage is done. It's already spread to other sites."

"But so has his resignation." She shows me her phone. *Congressional Candidate resigns over attack on opponent's teenage daughter.*

"That's a site friendly to Mom, though. There'll be more."

Mel sighs and starts texting. "What are you doing?" I ask.

"Texting Jared back. I don't blame *him*. He's

probably the one who talked his dad into pulling out of the race."

I don't say anything. It's kind of loud.

"He didn't mean to hurt you," Mel says, looking up at me. "You know that, don't you?"

I run my fingers across the top of her bedspread. "You're more important. This is way bigger than *my* stupid thing." She looks at me. "You see? That's what I mean. The pity. That's what I don't want or need and you just have to stop."

Mel's phone buzzes. I assume it's Jared texting back, but it's not. "Steve's shift doesn't start until midnight," Mel says, getting up. "I'm going to go see him. Get some smartness and squeezing."

I get up and hug her. "I'd kill anybody who tried to hurt you," I say.

She hugs me back. "Not if I was too busy killing them first."

After she leaves, I press a number on my phone.

"Can you come over?" I say.

"Absolutely," says Henna.

oOo

304

We sit on the edge of my bed in a surprisingly nice kind of silence.

"You're not all right," she finally says.

"No," I say. "I said some things to Jared. He said some things to me."

"Bad things?"

"End of friendship things."

"I'm sure that isn't true," Henna says. "I'm sure it isn't–"

"Don't *pity* me," I nearly snap. "Jesus, why does everyone–?"

I stop because my eyes are filling up. Again. This is ridiculous.

"I think you're wrong about that." Henna puts a single finger on my chin and makes me turn my head to her. It's kind of funny. We both smile, but mine doesn't last. "I think you mistake care for pity," she says. "We worry about you."

"Same thing."

"No, it isn't. We worry about Mel, too. And you worry about me and so does Mel. It's care, Mike. Who have we got to rely on except each other? For example, this isn't pity."

She kisses me. I'm so surprised I barely kiss her back.

"I don't do pity kisses," she says. "I don't do pity *anything*. Pity is patronizing. Pity is an assumption of superiority."

"That sounds like your dad."

"It *is* my dad, but he's right. He says kindness is better. Kindness is the most important thing of all. Pity is an insult. Kindness is a miracle."

"So you're kissing me out of kindness?"

"No," she says, frowning. "I'm kissing you because I've always wanted to, Mike. You never let me."

"I never *let* you–?"

"We're each other's questions, aren't we? The question that never gets an answer."

"What do you mean–?"

But she's already kissing me again.

This time I'm definitely kissing her back.

No one's home. My mom went to handle her lawyers and dropped Meredith off at a Saturday horseback-riding lesson (the first, it's a new thing). Dad is at work or wherever. And Mel's out with

Steve. There's no one in the house except for me and Henna.

Then she pulls my shirt off over my head, and there's no one in the *world* except me and her.

CHAPTER THE TWENTIETH, *in which Satchel and second indie kid Finn close nearly every fissure the Immortals have made; "I love you," Finn says, before they close the final one in the basement of the school on the morning of graduation; Satchel realizes that Finn was her true love all along; they finally kiss, but then the Court of the Immortals emerges through the fissure; Satchel and Finn run out of the building, but the Prince of the Immortals kills second indie kid Finn; overcome with grief, Satchel is dragged back down under the school by the Prince to perform the final ceremony once and for all.*

◄O►

On graduation day, it's about nine hundred degrees. So thank God we get to wear long black gowns and hats on the football field for a couple hours.

The last few days have been a blur, a tough, weird blur. I haven't spoken to Jared, even though he's called me and texted me a bunch of times, apologizing for saying what he said. I texted back saying I was sorry, too.

But I didn't call.

We've been kind of set free from our classes the last two schooldays of this last school week. Senior privilege again, which you can take or not. I took it, going everywhere I could with Henna: the little northwest zoo just up the road, where we saw moose and elk panting in the sun; the bigger zoo in the town about an hour away, where a rhinoceros did the same; miniature golf again; the movies. Even just sitting in my room looking at our phones for hours on end. But doing it together.

Either way, I didn't go to school. Mel went, but she said Jared wasn't there either.

Mel's thing is still churning, my mom still fighting it, helped a lot by Mr Shurin dropping out of the race. Not helped by Cynthia deciding she's going to run instead. For most of the week, Mel's stayed over at

Steve's – who my parents now know the existence of and are seemingly in no position to argue that Mel wants to hang around him and not them – so I've barely seen her either, except over the phone on videos and chats.

Nothing more happened with the blue lights, though we're all worried that means we're leading up to something even bigger and more horrible that'll end it all.

"As long as we can graduate before they blow up the school," Henna said.

Because Henna.

Because Henna, because Henna, because Henna.

We slept together. It was everything I'd ever wanted, everything I'd ever hoped for, even the parts where I'd imagined we were in it together and it was something she wanted as much as I did and we were a team and it was for us both.

It was beautiful and amazing and so hot I've pretty much jerked off to it every day since (shut up, you would, too) and the way she smelled and the way her skin felt and the way we laughed sometimes (quite a lot over the condom) and the way we were serious other times and just the being there, in that way, her body against my body and mine against hers. It felt like my heart was breaking – and it *was* breaking, over Jared, over graduation, over everything – but it was okay because Henna Henna Henna...

It was all those things, and it was also more. Because we realized something, both of us.

We don't belong together as boyfriend and girlfriend.

"I think I see what you mean," I said to her, after, arms around each other. "About being each other's question."

"Yeah," she said. "It was the car accident that made me finally want to know the answer. You were there, holding my hand, and I thought, *Is it him? Is it really him?*"

"I've been asking myself that since we were kids."

"It always kept me from really committing to Tony. I kept thinking, in another life, if I made different choices, it could be you and me instead. I suppose I just got sick of expecting somebody else to give me the answer." She leaned up on one elbow. "I love you, Mike."

"I love you, too, Henna."

"And I loved *that*, what we just did. But this isn't us, is it?"

"No," I said. "I don't think it is."

"It's love. But it's a different kind."

"Doesn't make it any less love, though."

She lay back down and snuggled into me. "Just think, all this time we could have been each other's best friend."

"That would have been awesome."

"Still can be."

I smiled. "The spirit of exploration?"

I could almost feel her smiling back. "We could give it a shot."

And now I'm picking her up at her house, cast and all, cap and gown and all, on our graduation day. The graduation pairs are, for some reason, still old-fashioned boy-girl; it's long been the plan that I'll walk with Henna, and Mel will walk with Jared. Which will probably be fine.

"Big day," Henna says, getting into my car. She

shuts the door and looks back at her parents. Nobody waves to each other.

"What's going on?" I say, driving away.

"Later," she says, smiling. "This is a happy day. In a whole bunch of ways."

The ceremony's at noon. The sun is already baking the trees, making the whole world smell dusty. Mel is coming with Steve from his apartment. My mom's bringing Meredith later and will see us at the ceremony. My dad was so drunk he passed out in his office this morning in his work clothes and couldn't be woken. Me and Mel are just hoping he lives until rehab, though hopefully Mom will make sure of that.

Jared and his dad will be there. Which won't be awkward for anybody.

"It's going to be okay, Mike," Henna says, like she's reading my mind.

"You think so?"

"I mean everything," she says, looking out the window as we drive down the road to school for the millionth time. For the last time. "I think everything's going to be okay. All of it. All of *us*."

This makes my stomach hurt. I squirm in the

driver's seat so much, Henna notices. "Do you really believe in fate that much, Mikey? Do you really believe it exists only to punch you in the face?"

"It's done some pretty good punching so far."

She just looks back out her window. "I think it's going to be okay. Even you."

And I begin to count the telephone poles we pass.

I can't seem to stop.

–But then I do.

It's already pretty crowded when we get there, even though it's two full hours before the actual graduation part. We've got some sort of practice to get through first, though how hard can it be? We find Mel and Steve in the sea of sweating black robes. Jared and Nathan are with them. Henna hugs everybody.

"Hey," I say to Jared.

"Hey," he says.

Everyone's looking at us. "Oh, for God's sake," Mel says, grabbing each of us by the arm and pushing us towards the edge of the crowd. "Go. Work it out. It's our last day."

So we do. We walk away from the main field where graduation practice is starting – seriously, *practice* – and we head around to the back of the gym, away from where any teacher might spot us and drag us back.

"I'm sorry," Jared says, first thing.

"I'm sorry, too," I say.

"I didn't mean those things. I really didn't."

"You did, but ... I kind of deserved them."

"I kind of deserved them, too."

We don't say anything else for a minute.

"Is that it?" I ask, actually curious.

"I guess so."

"Are we okay?"

"Doesn't really feel like it, does it?"

Another long pause.

"I slept with Henna," I say.

He smiles, amazed. "You *did*?"

"Yeah. And we figured out we really are only just friends. It's been kind of ... kind of great, actually."

"See?" he says. "There's a secret you kept from *me*."

"I'd have a lifetime to go to catch up with you."

He looks away, trying to shove his hands in his pockets through his graduation robe. It doesn't work. "Yeah," he says. "I know. But Mikey, I fight with everything I've got to have a normal life. No one will ever let me. Except you. You've been the guy who saved me. Lots of times."

"You could tell me anything, Jared. Anything."

He winces, briefly. "It has nothing to do with not trusting you. It's to do with what something becomes once you tell it. It's like it's truer. And it's got a life of its own and it rushes out into the world and becomes something you can't control."

I wait for him to keep going. He does.

"I don't want to be an indie kid, Mike. I *should* be one. I'm gay. I'm part God. Jared isn't even my first name–"

"Mercury," I say, out loud for maybe the first time in ten years. He winces again. I really can't tell you how much he hates it.

"What chance do I have with a name like that? I just want a normal life. I want things that are *mine*. I want my own choices, not ones made for me even by people who mean well or are my friends."

"I wouldn't have made any choices about Nathan for you, one way or the other."

"I know. I do know that. I was wrong and I'm sorry." He shrugs. "But I finally meet somebody and now what? We've got the summer, but I'm moving away. All of us are."

"Mel's doing the same thing with Steve."

"I know."

I wait. And wait some more. "There's something else, isn't there?"

He takes a deep breath. "Mike, what would you say if I could–"

And we hear the moan from the bushes.

There's a row of ferns and shrubs behind the gym, mainly so the huge back fence with barbed wire on top looks slightly less like a huge back fence with barbed wire on top. The moan that came from them wasn't words; it was just a moan, low and guttural and wet-sounding.

"What was that?" I say, thinking of the mountain lion again, thinking also that we haven't yet seen the big finale for whatever mess the indie kids are mixed up in, so maybe there are more blue lights to come.

We hear it again. "There," Jared points, already moving over. I'm sweating like crazy in this stupid gown, and I can feel my clothes sticking to me as we cross into the sun again, over to the shrubs. We start pushing back leaves and branches, looking for where the noise came from, then right at my feet–

It's a boy. It's an indie kid.

"Oh, shit," Jared says.

I yank back the branches to get them out of the way. The indie kid is on his stomach, his head is turned to the side, and we see the blood that's come out of his mouth and down his chin. It's congealed, like he's been here for an hour or two. Jared motions for me to help turn him over. The indie kid calls out in pain when we do, though he's barely conscious.

We see why. "Oh, my God," I say.

The indie kid is all in black, like we are, but these are just his normal clothes. His shirt has been all torn up, and there are terrible, terrible wounds on his chest, all bleeding badly, like he's been stabbed over and over again. I'm amazed he's still alive, and

I think he just barely is. His eyes are only half-open, and he doesn't seem to know who we are or that we're even here.

"I know him," Jared says. "He's one of the Finns."

It *is* one of the Finns. I recognize him, too. "What does it mean?"

"I don't know."

I stand to get my phone out from under my robes. "We've got to get some help."

"I don't think we have time," Jared says, pushing up his sleeves.

"Can you heal him enough?" I ask. "Enough to keep him alive until–"

But Jared just gives me a look, one I can barely describe. It's regretful and sad, but it's also stern, like he has no choice.

"Jared?" I say.

He puts his hands on the indie kid.

Light comes from his palms, but it's like nothing I've ever seen from him before. It's much brighter, much bigger, and seems almost alive, snaking around the indie kid's body, disappearing into his wounds, into his mouth and eyes, too. Jared seems to be straining with effort and when he opens his own mouth to gasp, light pours from that, too. There's a sound that's half airplane engine, half windstorm–

And then it all stops.

"What the hell was that?" I ask.

Jared looks at me, grim. "The something else."

The indie kid takes a deep, choking breath and sits up, surprise leaking out everywhere on his face. He stares at me and Jared like we might be ghosts. "Jared?" he says. "Mike Mitchell?"

"That's us," Jared says.

The indie kid looks down at his shirt, torn, dark with blood–

But not a single wound anywhere.

"I don't think this was supposed to happen," the indie kid says, amazed. "I think I was supposed to die."

"You're welcome," I say.

"Thank you," he says.

"Everyone's *supposed* to die," Jared says. "You just weren't supposed to die right now."

The indie kid takes a deep breath. "I think you're wrong about that." He smiles, shaken. "But I'm glad you are."

"What happened?" Jared asks.

The indie kid looks at us, remembering. "The Immortals surprised us. They came through the last fissure–" He jumps up, suddenly. "Satchel!"

Jared and I look at each other. "We didn't find a satchel," I say.

"No, no." The indie kid stands. "I can help her now. In fact–"

He runs off towards the parking lot, fast as he can.

"Where are you going?" I shout after him.

"Home!" he shouts back. "I can get something from there! Maybe we can *force* the fissure to close!"

"Can we help?" Jared says.

"I don't think you're supposed to! But thanks!"

He turns and keeps running. We watch him go. "Doesn't he want to graduate?" I say.

Jared shrugs. "Indie kids," he says, as if that explains everything.

So here's what it is. The Gods want Jared to go full-time. With his grandmother retired in her realms and his mother AWOL somewhere raising money for snow leopards, the Gods feel the position has gone unfilled for too long.

They've wanted this for quite a while now, it turns out.

"That's where I've been on those Saturdays," Jared says, as we line up, two-by-two, to proceed to our seats. Jared and I have decided, screw it, we're going to walk together, and so are Mel and Henna. What rebels we are. (Still, though.) "Except for the ones lately with Nathan."

Nathan, being a late transfer in, is way down the line from us, paired up with this Estonian exchange student who, I'll be honest, I didn't even know went to our school.

"I kept saying no," Jared tells me, as "Pomp and Circumstance" starts to play over the football field where all our families are seated, waiting for us to arrive. "And I had intended to *keep* saying no. They kept offering me stuff to make me change my mind, but I always turned them down."

We're in the first third of the line and so we start filing onto the football field behind the top students, including our valedictorian, a girl called Bethany who has to give a speech and looks like she can't stop swallowing from nervousness.

"So what happened to change things?" I ask.

"The mountain lion," Jared says, serious. "I couldn't save her. I never want that to happen again. I said I'd consider doing it if they gave me full power to heal anyone I wanted to."

"So that's what you did to Finn?"

Jared nods, then looks me in the eye. "I was still thinking about it. It's my whole life changed, after all, and I was going to see what you thought of this final offer. But by using it just now, I kind of accepted the deal anyway."

We reach the back rows of seats, heading down the centre aisle. I see Mom and Meredith. I wave. I wave at Mr and Mrs Silvennoinen, too. I see Mr Shurin. He waves with an agonized expression on his face. I find myself waving back.

"What does this all mean?" I say. I'm already realizing, though. "You're not coming to college with me, are you?"

"Wrong," Jared says, then laughs at my expression. "That was *my* condition. I want to go to college.

I want to see what that's like. But after that…"

"After that, you're a full-time God."

"Looks that way," Jared says. "I'll ascend after I get my degree."

"A God with a degree in Mathematics?"

"A God of *cats* with a degree in Mathematics." Jared shakes his head. "My usefulness will know no bounds."

We head down our row after Henna and Mel, who have let us be, let us keep talking. We wait, standing, for everyone to arrive.

"Will we still be able to be friends?" I ask him.

He just looks at me.

The Frenchly Canadian voice of our Principal booms over the field, sounding as bored as ever. "Graduates," he says. "Take your seats, I suppose."

You don't need to hear the ceremony. God knows I don't hear much of it. The Principal purposely gets a few English clichés wrong to raise some gentle laughter. ("It will be, as one says, up to you to take the cow by the bell." See? Gentle.) Bethany gets through her speech without fainting. The jazz band plays a horn-heavy version of Bold freakin' Sapphire.

I sit there, feeling like someone's tipped me out of a helicopter into the middle of the ocean.

Jared. Gone. Four years from now, sure, but gone. He won't even be on the planet somewhere like his absent mom. He'll be in his realms. Literally unreachable.

"I hate it, too, Mikey," he says to me while they start handing out diplomas. "Do you know how lonely Gods are?"

"Then why do it?"

"Because Finn would be dead if I didn't."

And what can I do but nod?

Before I know it, Mel's name is called and she stands to go to the front. I rouse myself to cheer and then I really do cheer, because Mel made it. Hell, we all made it. At least this far. Mel was supposed to walk with Jared, so they call his name next and I cheer again even though it feels like my chest is going to explode. Henna moves over next to me and when they call her name, she hugs me, whispers in my ear, "I'm not going to Africa," and heads up the aisle to get her diploma, smiling back at me. Mel and Jared have waited for her just off the stage and even though they're not supposed to, they do the same when my name is called.

I stand, I turn to my mom and Meredith – the former taking photos, the latter screaming like I was in Bolts of Fire – and I wave again. I step up onstage, still feeling at sea, feeling like I've just lost sight of shore and though I'm swimming okay for now, I don't know how long I'll be able to keep it up.

"Congratulations," the Principal says, shaking my hand.

I take my diploma from him.

And that's it. That's how simple it is. I graduate.

I see my friends clapping, waiting for me. They hug me as a group when I get there, a whole bunch of arms around me. The four of us, my friends.

At the end.

Jared hugs me individually, too. "There's something more," he says. "Something good but big. If you'll let me."

"We're kind of holding up the line here," I say, stupidly, still reeling from all this new info.

"I don't care." He takes hold of my shoulders. "I can finally heal you, Mikey," he says, in the middle of all this graduating. "The OCD. The anxiety. Everything."

"But you can't. That's always been too complex–"

"I can. That was another of my conditions if I took the deal."

I don't know what to say to this. Henna and Mel are still there, watching, other graduates trying to squeeze around us, a number of them just staying and hugging their own friends because why the hell not? The music from the band is loud and endless.

"Could you heal Mel?" I say, not even knowing I was going to say it. "Could you make it so she's okay forever?"

Mel starts to cry when I say that, but in a good way, even though it's clear she's not at all sure what we're talking about. Jared just smiles. "See, Mikey? This is why you're never the least wanted. Not ever."

I see a teacher finally wading his way over to us to get us out of the way, as more and more students are hanging around beside us in front of the stage, waiting for even more friends, waiting to have last conversations.

Or first conversations, I guess. The first conversations of the new life.

"I waited for *this*," Jared says. "I asked for years and they said it was too much for my realm. It would give me advantages over too many other Gods, but I kept saying no."

"Until you finally said yes," I say.

"Until *they* finally said yes."

I think of his resignation about healing the indie kid, how he had no choice but to take the deal. He must read my thoughts.

"I thought it would be you," he says. "I thought it was you I would heal completely first, not Finn. But healing you meant I had to take the deal. Had to leave. And it was either seeing you suffer or leaving you behind."

"And now since you're leaving anyway..."

He shows me his palms. They light up. "This is how much you matter to me, Mikey."

I look up in his eyes. The day is hot, the crowd around us getting bigger, louder, that damn music still parping out from the eleventh grade brass band. Henna and Mel watching us. Even Nathan finally coming through the now quite uncontrollable crowd. My mom and sister out there somewhere. The future swirling in.

Suddenly a little less worrying.

"That's all I ever really wanted to know," I say, realizing right that second that it's absolutely true.

And then the girl I saw coming out of the gym after prom runs down the graduation aisle, not in a cap and gown.

"Everybody get out of here!" she screams, loud enough to be heard over all the noise. "The school is about to blow!"

CHAPTER THE TWENTY-FIRST, *in which they blow up the high school.*

◄O►

We watch the school burn, despite the best efforts of every fire truck within fifty miles.

The explosion took out nearly everything, including half the football field and nearly all of the parking lot. Most of our cars were destroyed, so no one's been able to quite get home yet. Blue lights flashed through the initial explosions – including a pillar that reached all the way up to the clouds – but then they stopped and it was just a ridiculously huge fire.

One that, as far as we can tell, didn't kill anyone. Not even any indie kids.

When that girl told everyone to run, everyone did, even the adults, who you would have thought would assume it was a prank. But maybe they really *could* sense that there was something wrong going on in the town. Or maybe they remember more about their own teenage years than they ever let on.

Even my mom, carrying Meredith, found us in what turned out to be our second stampede of the month.

"Should we take her seriously?" she asked.

"We really should," Mel said, dragging her along.

Everybody ran. Everybody got to a safe distance. Everybody was able to watch as the gym exploded in a wave so strong, it still knocked us back.

And that was the end of our high school. Which was only eight years old, because it had replaced the last one that had been blown up to destroy the soul-eating ghosts. The circle of life, I guess.

There are small hills to one side of the school. They're fairly wooded, but you can still get a good view of the fire through the trees. There's also a fast-food place at the bottom of the other side, down from the Mexican place where we ate lunch so many times, and after everyone realized we weren't dead or likely to be, a lot of us were hungry. We got burgers and fries and climbed back up the hill to watch the blaze. We're surrounded now by students in their caps and gowns, parents in suits and dresses, a few news crews – who are talking to my mother, but she's keeping them a safe distance from me and Mel and Henna and Jared and Nathan and Steve and Meredith (who my mom left with us) – as we sit and eat and watch our high school burn to the ground.

"Well," Mel says, taking a bite of a chicken burger, even eating the bun, "at least *we* got our diplomas."

"I'm sure everyone else will have theirs mailed to them," Jared says. He's unzipped his gown and is wearing it like a cape. Still got the cap on, though. We all do. Because why not? We graduated.

"Think Dad can get us some cars for the summer?" I ask.

"As payment for missing the ceremony?" Mel says. "Oh, yeah. Henna and Jared and Nathan, too. Though, actually, if he'd come today, he might not have been able to run fast enough, so maybe it's for the best."

"I can't believe they blew up the school," Nathan

says, his head resting on Jared's stomach.

Henna drinks the last of her soda. "I know. It felt so inevitable, you kind of thought it would never actually happen."

"As long as they rebuild it by the time *I* graduate," Meredith says.

"I'm sure they will, Merde Breath," Jared says. "They can only have really good insurance, you'd think."

"Don't call me that," Meredith says.

"You know we mean it with love, don't you, Bite Size?" Jared asks her.

"Yeah," she says, smiling. "That's why I keep hoping you will. So I can keep saying, 'Don't call me that.'"

"Weirdo," Mel says, affectionately, and hands some more fries to our sister.

The sun's still out, but it's late afternoon. We've been here a couple hours, and the fire guys are still no closer to having it under control. Fortunately, the school's in the middle of a huge clearing, so there's not much chance of the forest catching. That would *really* suck.

Instead, it's like a town-sized picnic. We wave to people we know as they walk by or come up to us and chat. We've all found our parents and figured out we're all safe. I even let Mr Shurin give me a hug. "I can't tell you how sorry I am," he said.

"You don't need to," I said back.

He let us be and started walking the couple miles back to his house, his car having been toasted, too. I feel bad for him, despite also wanting to kill him for involving Mel. But he's not a loser. He's never been a loser. And his only family is leaving for college. And after that, leaving forever, as far as I understand it. What's he going to have left?

What are any of us?

"You okay?" Jared says, frowning at me now.

"Just thinking," I say.

We're lying on a grassy stretch. Graduation robes turn out to make decent picnic blankets, though I doubt we'll get our deposits back. Jared gently scoots Nathan off his stomach. Nathan takes the hint and turns his full attention to Henna. Which, all right, is nice of him.

"I really could, Mike," Jared says. "Heal you."

"I know. I saw it with Finn."

"I want to. I've always hated seeing you suffer."

I look at him. I don't answer. He straightens up suddenly. "Oh, my God," he says. "I'm such an idiot." He turns to Henna. "Can I see your arm?"

Surprised, she holds it out to him. "Why?"

I'm still a little surprised myself she doesn't know already. Then I'm kind of pleased. No one else knew. He told me first.

"Do you mind if I totally heal this?" Jared asks her.

"Can you *do* that?"

"I can now." He puts his palms on her cast. The white lights shoot out briefly one more time and stop. Henna flexes her hand at the end of her cast and frowns.

"It doesn't feel weird any more," she says. "You healed the whole thing?" She grabs some loose plaster at the end of the cast, which is looking pretty grimy. "Think I can take this off?"

"Wait, wait," Steve says, sitting up. "What the hell's going on? You can't just take off a–"

But Henna's already ripping at the rough plaster.

Nathan helps her, and they get it off pretty quickly. She rolls her hand around. "It's healed," she says. "It's completely healed." She turns her whole wrist around and looks at Jared. "You even fixed the scar."

They all look at me. My hand goes up to my own scar. "I thought you guys said you liked it."

"What's going on?" Steve asks again.

Mel takes his hand gently. "I told you," she says. "You're going to have to have an open mind around us."

"But if he can do that—"

"Think of all the other good I can do," Jared says. Then he says, more quietly, so only I can hear. "Until I ascend."

I feel the pang in my stomach again. That's still there. Jared going away forever. He hasn't told the others about this yet either. For now, it's just me and him knowing. I finally understand what a burden a secret can be.

Tony Kim walks through some trees, sees us and comes over. Henna stands and throws her arms around him. "Thank God, you're okay," she says. He barely recovers his surprise in time to hug her back. "Come," she says, taking his hand. "Sit with us."

He sits down next to her on her graduation gown and they instantly fall into deep conversation.

Henna's not going to Africa. She told me while we waited in the disaster-swollen line at the fast-food place. "I'm eighteen," she said. "I realized they can't actually make me. It was only a matter of willpower." She shrugged. "I stayed nice through the whole thing. I never yelled or went crazy. I just said it was my last summer to see you, that the Central African Republic was too dangerous for *any* of us to go, and that I needed to start making important decisions for myself."

"What'd they say?" I asked.

"What could they say? I was right."

Strangely, the first reaction they had was to try for a compromise. They agreed the Central African Republic and its civil war was probably not the wisest choice, so how about Romania?

"Romania?" I said, surprised. "Does Romania need missionaries? Or foot specialists?"

"They've got the Romanian Orthodox Church

and, as far as I know, hospitals. So, no, not really. But they want to go anyway."

"And?"

She smiled at me, more relaxed than I've ever seen her. "I said no."

I watch her and Tony talk now. I watch the closeness they have. I watch the way he won't stop looking into her eyes and she won't stop looking into his and the way they touch each other here and there and I bet she's got the desire feeling in her stomach for him. I bet he's got it for her, too. Will they end up together and getting married? Who knows? But looking at them, I'm not even jealous.

I'm happy.

Which is the weirdest thing of all.

"That's the guy!" we hear and see the still-alive Finn coming up with the girl who warned us all. She gets *all* kinds of looks from people she passes, but she ignores them. They come straight over to Jared and she throws a hug around him. "Oof," he says.

"You saved him," she says. "That wasn't supposed to happen, but you did."

"She was going to have to sacrifice herself to

save us," Finn says. "But because of you, I could help her and we destroyed the fissures of the Immortals once and for all!"

There's a silence.

"Am I allowed to say, *What the hell are you talking about* this time?" Steve asks.

"You know what?" Mel says. "All I really want to know is if it's over."

The girl, who I remember now is called Satchel – which explains why Finn was asking for a satchel earlier – blows out a long breath and nods. "Yeah," she says. "It's over."

"Thank goodness," Mel says, seriously.

Satchel and Finn stand there, looking a little lost.

"Where are the other indie kids?" I ask.

She looks confused. "The other who?"

"I think that's what they call us," Finn says to her.

"Really?" She seems genuinely surprised. Then she looks around the woods. "I'm not sure, actually. We've all got kind of scattered." Her chin crumples up a bit. "And not all of us made it."

"Hey," Mel says, kindly. "It's okay."

"I'm sorry for all this," Satchel says, through

tears. "I don't know why it always happens to us. I don't know why *we* always have to blow up the high school–"

"Don't worry about it," Mel says, making a space for Satchel and Finn to sit. "Everybody's got something."

"Ain't that the truth?" Jared says.

Satchel and Finn sit. We all, all of us, together, watch the school still burn.

"You know what?" I say, quietly, to Jared.

"What?"

"I think... I think I don't want you to heal my scar. Or anything else yet."

"You sure?"

"Yeah. If it gets bad again. Bad enough to... Well, I'll think about it then. But not yet."

"Is the medication working that well?"

"No, but if you heal all that stuff, I'll live the rest of my life not knowing if I could have figured it out on my own."

He nods, solemnly. "That makes sense. In fact, what do you wanna bet that's what your sister will say, too?"

I smile at that. "That you offered, Jared. That you bargained. For *me*..." I find that I can't go on.

He knows what I mean. "I'm always here for you," he says. "If you need it."

"For another four years," I say, wiping my eyes.

"Four years is a long time. A lot could happen."

"Maybe."

And as I put my own hand up to feel my scar, I think he's right. A lot *could* happen. Mel and Steve could stay together. Or not. Henna and Tony could get back together. Or not. Me and Jared could stay firm friends. Or we could drift apart. Maybe there's a chance even the God stuff will change. Maybe Nathan will get run over by a bus that I'm not anywhere near. Maybe I'll come off my medication. Or stay on it. Maybe my mom *won't* win her race after all. Maybe my dad will become a new person and what will that be like? What will this *summer* be like?

Too fast, probably. Too many nights at Grillers, but also nights together, all of us. Like we are now.

I look at us. Jared and Mel, who I'm so proud of, and Henna and Meredith and Steve and even Nathan and even the two indie kids, who really do seem just like the rest of us. Just normal people, having a burger above the crater where their school once was.

"What metaphor are we going to use for this?" Nathan asks. "Our childhoods burning down?"

"I think our childhoods burnt down a long time ago," Mel says, leaning against Steve.

"High school is like living through fire?" Henna suggests.

"That's kind of true," I say.

"What about, from the ashes, phoenixes will rise?" Meredith suggests.

"That sounds too much like hard work, Merde Breath," Jared says. "I think it's just a high school that burnt down. I don't think it's a metaphor at all."

"Spoilsport," Nathan says. They laugh together. And I'm only a little bit jealous.

"Why does everything have to *mean* something, though?" Jared asks. "Haven't we got enough life to be living?"

But then, nodding at the tower of smoke that stretches up against the Mountain – it's actually kind of beautiful – I say, "Everything's always ending. But everything's always beginning, too."

"God," Henna says, "that would have been a *much* better prom theme than 'Forever Young'."

We stay watching the fire, which probably *is* just a fire, but we watch it together. Me and my friends. And there'll be a tomorrow, of course there will, when it all begins again. But right now is almost a kind of loop for me, something to feel on the inside of, but this time it's good. It's a loop with my friends that would even be a pretty damn good forever.

I know, if I need it, they'll save me.

I also know that I might not need it quite so often.

We watch the fire. We watch the fire.

And still we watch.

AUTHOR'S NOTE

Shortly after the devastating Typhoon Haiyan, the YA authors Keren David, Candy Gourlay and Keris Stainton (who you should all read) set up Authors for the Philippines, a fund-raising drive for the Red Cross. Authors donated various prizes for which people bid. It was wildly successful – raising over £55,000 – and I was very proud to be a part of it.

I auctioned off the chance to have the winner's name in this book, and I became the luckiest author in the world when the auction was won by Henna Silvennoinen, a name so amazing and gorgeous I want to use it in every book from now on. Henna the character was new on the page and looking for a name; Henna the person gave her the perfect one.

Coming in second place in the auction was a friend called Jared Shurin. Wanting to help out the good cause, Jared and I agreed that if he made his donation to the Red Cross anyway, he could be in the book, too (mainly because I liked the name Jared so much for the character, who up until then had been a non-committed "Josh").

Needless to say, the characters and the real people only have their names in common, and any other similarities are coincidental, as book characters grow into lives of their own. Though I know for a fact the real Jared Shurin now has business cards that say, "Three-quarters Jewish, one-quarter God."

ABOUT PATRICK NESS

Photo © Helen Giles 2013

Patrick Ness was born in the USA, but has lived in London since 1999.

He writes both novels and short stories for adults and children, but is best known for his books for young adults. His first books for teenagers made up the Chaos Walking trilogy, of which the first book, *The Knife of Never Letting Go*, won the Guardian Children's Fiction Prize and the Booktrust Teenage Prize, followed by *The Ask and the Answer*, which won the Costa Award. All three titles in the trilogy were shortlisted for the prestigious Carnegie Medal, an unprecedented event, and in 2011 the third title, *Monsters of Men*, won the award.

Patrick's sixth book, *A Monster Calls*, was based on an original idea by Siobhan Dowd and illustrated by Jim Kay. It won every major prize in children's fiction, including the Galaxy National Book Award, the UKLA Book Award and the Red House Children's Book Award. In 2012 it became the first book ever to win both the Carnegie Medal and the Kate Greenaway Medal. Patrick has also written the screenplay for the film of *A Monster Calls*. Directed by Juan Antonio Bayona and starring Liam Neeson, Sigourney Weaver and Felicity Jones, the film is set for release in 2016.

In 2013 he published his next novel *More Than This* to great critical acclaim. It was also shortlisted for the Carnegie Medal.

Enjoyed this book? Tweet us your thoughts.
#TheRestofUs   @Patrick_Ness   @WalkerBooksUK